picking off new shoots will not stop the spring

witness poems and essays
from Burma/Myanmar
1988–2021

edited by ko ko thett and brian haman

"WARNING: There's blood everywhere in these pages. That's as it should be. The book in your hands bears witness to the long, bloodstained struggle against military oppression by the people of Myanmar/Burma. Here is an anthology exceptional in impact and importance, not least because the poets and writers serving as witnesses have themselves fought and died at the frontlines of resistance.

Picking off new shoots will not stop the spring brings together for the first time in print—in translations both inspired and felicitous—poet-heros of the '88 Uprising, new voices from within the Chin, Kachin and Rohingya minorities, young poet-warriors of the ongoing armed struggle, and early martyrs of the Spring Revolution, notably K Za Win and Khet Thi. Together they raise a cri de coeur of resistance, resilience, and—through their poetry—redemption."

—Wendy Law-Yone
Author of *Golden Parasol: A Daughter's Memoir of Burma,*
The Road to Wanting, Irrawaddy Tango and *The Coffin Tree*

"With poems and essays ranging from optimistic zeal to righteous rage, Myanmar's writers have responded to the death and destruction wrought by the 2021 coup with prose imbued with birth, rebirth, and revolution. The powerful voices in this inspiring anthology demands that we all keep fighting for a free and just Myanmar, and reminds us that 'If we retreat this time, we will have to live in defeat forever'."

—Aye Min Thant
Features editor, *Frontier Myanmar*

"From the Yoma foothills to the Chindwin river, Monywa to Cox's Bazaar, the voices in this searing new collections map a rich wilderness of witness. Kachin, Nepal, Burmese, Rohingya, Shan, Sino-Burmese and other voices mourn the murdered, the disappeared, and light a pyre for a vanished future. Spanning more than forty years of resistance since the iconic student protests of 8 August 1988 to the nationwide protests and murderous mayhem that followed the military coup of February 2021, these writings offer more than witness. Through lullabies, battle-cries, memes, digital memorials, kitchen cacophonies, protective prayers, odes to flip flops, roadside burials and prison cells, they redefine poetic justice. An elegy to democracy, an artists' manifesto and a rejection of the moral bankruptcy of a corrupt military, Ko Ko Thett and Brian Haman's urgent new anthology demands our attention."

—Penny Edwards
Associate Professor, Southeast Asian Studies, UC Berkeley

Balestier Press
Centurion House, London TW18 4AX
www.balestier.com

Picking Off New Shoots Will Not Stop the Spring:
Witness poems and essays from Burma/Myanmar (1988–2021)
Edited by Ko Ko Thett and Brian Haman
Copyright © Ethos Books, 2022
Copyrights to individual works, translations and photos featured in this
publication are reserved by their respective authors and translators.

First published in Singapore by Ethos Books
This edition first published in UK by Balestier Press in 2022

A CIP catalogue record for this book is available from the British Library.

ISBN 978 1 913891 23 7

Photo credits:
"bullet hole in the bamboo wall" (frontispiece) by anonymous
"Dr Thiha Tin Tun's will" (p16) by Dr Thiha Tin Tun
"Khet Thi's poem" (p148) by Chaw Su
"Min Lu's poem" (p216) by Yu Ya

Cover art by Black ART
Cover design by Lee Wen-yi
Layout and design by Pagesetters Services Pte Ltd

Contents

SECTION II: 2020–2010

SECTION III: 2010–1988

EPILOGUE

Introduction

Ko Ko Thett & Brian Haman

Generosity, altruism and courage are the backbone of any struggle against tyranny. In the wake of the military's overthrow of Myanmar's democratically elected government in February 2021, we found the online literary outpouring of outrage, grief and dissent particularly generous, altruistic and courageous.

This marshalling of the digital space for the purpose of activism, protests and resistance is all the more remarkable considering the fact that Myanmar "came online" virtually overnight. Until the mid-2000s, most people in the country did not have access to the internet or even to mobile phones.

Over the course of the past ten years, however, an increase in internet freedom and access resulted in the widespread adoption of mobile devices. A greater openness seemed to speak to a "transitional Myanmar", one characterised by efforts to reintegrate the country into the global economy. After five decades of international, economic and political isolation, there even appeared to be overtures to constitutional democracy and judiciary reform.

Myanmar's transition was far from fair, as demonstrated by the glaring political and economic disparities between haves and have-nots. The most hideous examples emerged in the form of the ethnic cleansing of the Rohingya in the western Rakhine littoral and the war against Kachin peoples in the north.

And what little progress that Myanmar enjoyed has once again ground to an abrupt halt, with the military yet again nipping democracy in the bud. Since then, the subversion of democratic elections, mass arrests, imposition of house arrest for elected politicians, ethnic and religious divisiveness, extreme physical and psychological torture, sexual- and gender-based violence, censorship and the heavy use of lethal and often indiscriminate force with virtual impunity have become the new normal in the country.

By September, guerrilla journalists from Myanmar reported that some of the military-occupied towns in ethnic Chin and Karenni regions became completely devoid of souls, with thousands of residents internally displaced. As if this were not enough, millions in Myanmar are facing growing food insecurity amid poverty, political unrest, and economic crisis. And then there are the devastating consequences of the COVID-19 pandemic, which has only compounded the negative shocks that have ravaged the country as it lurches under the weight of the junta.

Despite the bloodshed, the seemingly endless cycles of violence and trauma and the countless innocents who are no longer with us, poetry—and writing more generally—continues to play an important role in the country's Civil Disobedience Movement. Given the ephemeral nature of the online environment along with the reality of internet outages, throttling and outright censorship, so much of this writing remains either undocumented, untranslated or entirely inaccessible. This book was thus initially conceived as an anthology of poems and essays—first-hand accounts from the ensuing protests.

There was an urgently felt need to preserve these online writings in a more durable and enduring format. Not only does this corpus of writing demonstrate the power and possibilities of the written word when faced with the barrel of a gun, but it also reveals Burmese writing to be aesthetically accomplished and significant. In this respect, witness writings from Myanmar should not be understood merely as a local phenomenon with only local relevance, but rather seen within the international context of recent resistance art movements.

The initial essays and poems we received in February and early March, largely via PEN Myanmar, brimmed with hope for a non-violent people's revolution. By the end of March, the military had already started to react to these largely peaceful protests with astonishing violence.

Among the dead was a teenage girl wearing an "Everything will be OK" T-shirt. She had been shot in the head, an alarmingly common fate shared by many of her fellow protesters. Earlier in the month, the brutal killing of two poets, Myint Myint Zin and K Za Win, sent shock waves through the country and international community. Myint Myint Zin (also known as Kyi Lin Aye) was a teacher and poet who was well loved by her students. K Za Win was a celebrated poet who spent over a year in jail as a student for his advocacy of educational reforms. Many poets such as Maung Yu Py, Han Lynn, and Moe Oo Swe Nyein, among others, have been jailed for taking part in the protests. We are honoured to include poems by a number of these poets, including some best-loved poems by Khet Thi who died at the hands of the junta's inquisitors on 8th May.

Horrified, angered or simply exasperated by the increasingly authoritarian military regime and its murderous actions, civilians in Myanmar began fighting back with whatever means they had. Some banged pots and pans at night, while others tended to the injured or provided shelter to the hunted. The writing in this collection reflects this spirit of ingenuity, resourcefulness and defiance.

There is, for example, an essay describing the harrowing escape of a Kachin rights activist, another about the perils of withdrawing cash from a bank under the threat of the COVID-19 pandemic and the junta's ever-present surveillance, and yet another on a seemingly mundane piece of footwear, the flip-flop, which has a decades-long symbolic value in Myanmar's various protest movements. The discarded footwear on the streets of Myanmar signalled impromptu military violence as panicked protesters fleeing bullets sought refuge.

In a country mired in censorship since its very first military coup in 1962, people have had to adapt quickly to the hard-won online and offline freedoms of the 2010s. Veteran journalist Hanthawaddy U Win Tin has said that the side effects of censorship continued to weigh on Burmese writers following the easing of restrictions, but things seem to have changed for the digital generations, who have come of age in the 1990s and 2010s under a far different digital landscape. As such we have dedicated a special section featuring essays and poems from 2010 to 2020, mainly by youth and women writers, in order to showcase what was possible without the weight of censorship. Thanks to the Rohingya poet Mayyu Ali, we received some witness poems from the refugee camps and beyond, three of which are featured here.

The book is organised in reverse chronological order, suggesting the extent to which Myanmar has regressed—a temporal, economic, moral and political slippage that will likely reverberate through generations from now. The final section (2010–1988) features poems by dissidents, Min Ko Naing and Hanthawaddy U Win Tin, which have been capably translated by Kenneth Wong, and a long-form poem by Min Lu, for which the poet and his collaborators spent several years in jail, as well as a poem written in English by the exile poet activist and political economist Kyi May Kaung.

Perhaps this longer view will also give us pause to consider the implications of this inter-generational transmission and experience of everyday political violence in Myanmar, as a younger generation of writers, in some ways overwhelmed by the narratives that preceded them, must now bear witness to their own psychic wounds. In this respect, one is reminded of Primo Levi and the power of bearing witness despite the apparent inadequacy of language to communicate one's experiences or encapsulate one's memories.

And finally, we use the term "witness poems and essays" as distinct from "protest" or "resistance poems and essays". All protest writings may be witness writings but not all witness writings are protest writings. Witness writing, in our opinion, is more subjective and does not usually have an explicit political agenda—however politicised it might be or become. We would like to caution that violent imagery and emotionally laden strong language may be inevitable in some witness writings about physical, sexual or emotional abuses, atrocities and armed conflicts.

Despite the military's subversion of democratic elections, mass arrests, jailing of politicians, extreme physical and psychological cruelty, sexual- and gender-based violence, censorship and the heavy use of lethal and often indiscriminate force with virtual impunity, the hearts of the people of Myanmar continue to burn—sadder, but perhaps, indomitably wiser and more resolute.

It's time for the witnesses to speak for themselves.

These are their stories.

Dr Thiha Tin Tun's will

2021

We do not put our faith in skills,
We put our faith in the gun.

Tin Moe (1933–2007)

Zeyar Lynn

Myanmar

after China by Bob Perelman

We live as easy prey for the empire.
Numberless zero (that's us).
They tell the generals what to do.
The guy who told the gang to stage a coup was
very gong hsi but no fa tsai.
It's the year of the ox. We are boxed oxen billed for the kill.
If the brain you miss, aim at the heart.
The bullet blows your life off. The bastard son rises also.
I'd rather the world not issue statements;
Let us be killed in peace. Die in front of your life.
A stepfather who points at the gun at least
once every whim is a good stepfather.
The landscape is bloody-fucked.
The train sinks you in the drain. Slippages in the slaughter.
Folks marching along vast stretches of emptiness,
heading towards martyrdom.
Don't forget what your body looks like
when you are nowhere around your body.
Cots in the nursery caged up like coots,
gunned up and gunned down
where the generation would normally be.
Even the flags flying at the UN make Myanmar a fucking farce.
If it's time to die we get bullets.
They taste sweet to us. They Taste Sweet to us.
The guns are glowing. They point at us.

Pick up your body.
"Hey guess what?" "What?" "I've learned how to be shot and kill
"Damn! Why do some have all the luck?"
The person whose head exploded laughed at the bullet.
As the country fell, what could the world do?
Scavenge for loot? Slipped dreams.
The sniper looks great in uniform.
And the flag looks fucked too.
Nobody enjoyed their own deaths.
Time to rise up.
But better get used to mayhem too.

First published in *Jacket 2*, also in *Voice & Verse*, Summer 2021.
Zeyar Lynn is a poet, critic, writer, translator and language instructor who lives in Yangon. He has instigated a wider appreciation of postmodern and L=A=N=G=U=A=G=E poetry forms in Burmese, and is widely regarded as one of the most influential living poets in Burma.

K Za Win (1982-2021)

Skulls

Revolution will be in bloom
only when air, water and earth—
all the nutrients are in agreement.

Before the Revolution opened out,
a bullet blew someone's brains out,
out on the street.
Did that skull have a message for you?

Faced with the devil
is this or that statement relevant?

In the dharma of dha
you can't just wave the sword.
Step forward and cut them down!

The Revolution won't materialise
out of your mere thoughts.
Like blood, one must rise.

Don't ever waver again!
The fuse of the Revolution
is either you or myself!

First published in *Adi Magazine*, Summer 2021.
This is the final poem, dated 23.02.2021, by K Za Win (1982–2021),
who was shot dead by Myanmar security forces at a protest in Monywa
on 3 March 2021.

Moe Oo Swe Nyein

A revolutionary family

Father takes to the street
in his own guild.
Big Daughter takes to the street
in her own gang.
By eight in the afternoon,
Two Little Daughters will
bang pots and pans in protest.
For protection, Mother recites
verses from the Paritta and
goes online to spread the news.
When they hear injustice
the whole family will cuss at the dictator—
in one voice.

Moe Oo Swe Nyein is one of the poets snatched by security forces at a protest in Yangon on 27 March 2021. Before his arrest, he had edited and published a mini-anthology of Myanmar Spring Revolution poems and distributed it online. He was released from Insein prison, along with other poets and artists, in July 2021. The poem is dated 10 March 2021.

Mi Chan Wai

Residual lives

Come night
insecurity arrives on its toes
with a pair of peeping eyes
through bamboo mesh walls.

*

Baby cries, singalongs,
dog howls and caterwauls—
all those familiar noises are gone.
Between the dome of the firmament
and the roof of our homes
only the crows caw, over and over again.

*

Moles, fingers, saboteurs, dalan,
words that are news to me.

*

Foe has no label
written on his forehead.
But he is close.
Very close.

*

In the depth of the night
when all lights are out

everyone must hold their breath.
First the footsteps of the army boots,
then the orders,
"Two from this house!" "Three from that house."
"Pull'em down. Beat'em up!"
Rabid dogs snatch our neighbours.
The dalan, a finger whose moral flesh
is infested with maggots, is there to help.

*

A bullet out of the darkness
is blind, and will hit a random target.
It will destroy everything in its path.
At a corner of this world
a most violent plot unfolds
out of a tragic opera.

*

Comes the next morning
a group of remaining women
from the neighbourhood
take to the streets to witness the truth.

*

Their mouths will speak up.
Their hands will stretch.
They will pawn their own lives
for their husbands and sons
who have fallen
on that blood-stained asphalt road.

*

By eight pm
with their residual voices
they will bang pots and pans
in protest,
until
they hear the footsteps and
the finger again.

"Dalan", a Burmanised Hindi word, refers to any collaborator with the military regime, a snitch or a spy.

First published in *Adi Magazine*, Summer 2021.

Mi Chan Wai (1953) was born in Tha Htone in Mon State of Myanmar. In 1984, she wrote her first short story "I, the raft man" under her current penname, Mi Chan Wai, for *Myeik Magazine*. Since then she has continued to publish stories in various Burmese literary journals featuring the lives of fishermen, divers and their families from the Myeik archipelago. In 2000, she received the Myanmar National Literary Award for her collection of sea stories, *Heart Broken Oyster and Other Sea Short Stories*.

Dialogue Partner

Two words I hate most

It's neither seconds, minutes or hours,
nor days, weeks, months, or years, but decades!
For decades we have been thrashed
with a psychosomatic disorder.

No action has been taken against
the perpetrators. Time and again,
you "demand" and you "urge"
they respect our rights, whatever.

Like a series of natural disasters,
our decimation came in waves,
We have been washed ashore
on the land of lamentations.

Our exit towards wellbeing remains obscure.
You assume it's only dramatisation?
Can you guarantee non-repatriation?

Or have you been planning to exile us
further on the Island of Bhasan Char?
In the meantime I hear you
"demand", you "urge" whatever.

See with my eyes, think with my mind,
and feel with my heart for a second.
If you were me, you would definitely be

desperate to die, rather than survive.

I have a heart that beats and feels
pain and pleasure like yours. The same
blood flows in my veins as does in yours.

Tell me now, where is your empathy
your power, and your action
beyond "urge" and "demand" whatever?

Dialogue Partner (born 1990) is a Rohingya poet from Buthidaung
Township, Rakhine State, Myanmar.

Ma Thida

Picking off new shoots will not stop the spring

TEEN GIRLS IN WHITE TOPS and jeans confidently hold a placard that reads, "Picking off leaves won't stop the spring." Their faces show neither anger nor sorrow; they look determined. They are also shouting, "We are youths, we have a future." They don't believe in anger or sadness, but they do believe in hope. That group of teen girls belongs to tens of thousands of young people out on the streets in big and small cities—more than three hundred all over Myanmar.

Of course, they have hope. They voted in the general election in November 2020, mainly for the NLD (National League for Democracy). They are the five million strong of first-time voters. Not all of them were happy with the NLD government during the four years prior to the election. However, most of them had voted for the NLD, and are now calling for the release of Aung San Suu Kyi and president U Win Myint. They also carry banners that demand, "Free Our Leaders", "Respect Our Votes". They must have been overjoyed at having the chance to vote for the first time as responsible citizens. How can they be happy if their votes are not respected or recognised? Their fight against the junta is not for the political party they voted for, but simply for their votes and their rights.

A light truck is parked under the sun. Middle-aged men pack noodles into disposable lunch boxes, while a young man distributes lunch boxes to protestors under the shade of an overpass. Three teen girls in Nike caps, trainers and fancy dresses carry blue bin bags to collect throwaways directly from the hands of people and rubbish from the street. Three muscular men wait at a corner with their three-wheeled carts to dispose of refuse. The placards attached in front of their carts say, "We are no municipal workers. We are volunteers." On the other side of the road, out from the boot of a new SUV, some smart young men announce, "Water and fresh juices available here! Take what you want, and leave your garbage here in this box."

At another corner, a group of young people are working on the placards tailor-made to the demands. "Draw the three-finger sign for me." "I want a CDM lettering." "*Free Our Leaders!* for me please." Next to them, is an ambulance that reads, "For medical emergencies." Young doctors and nurses eat lunch from anonymous donors on the street while waiting for anyone who needs medical care. Some street boys and girls are enjoying a variety of free meals and drinks, receiving food packages and stowing them away in their worn-out backpacks. Some of them also collect empty bottles. None of the street kids are treated badly by anyone. When a 10-year-old street vendor girl expresses that she would like to offer her watermelon to the protestors, a young boy enables her charitable spirit by paying for half of all her costs. They look at each other with big smiles. Rich people politely collect rubbish from poor protestors and they appreciate each other's roles.

Those scenes are now the new normal on the streets of Myanmar. From 8 am in the morning until 5 pm in the evening, tens of thousands of people are out on the streets. After 5 pm, when the protests are over, no rubbish is left behind on the streets. From now on, the people of Myanmar might be reluctant to throw rubbish casually on the streets. A Spring Revolution, still going strong after three weeks and with no sign of abating, has introduced a new self-disciplined lifestyle to all generations and social groups.

Almost a month into the protests and there is no division based on class, gender, race or religion. No bad words, no bad behaviour, no looking down, no personal appraisals. There were almost no car accidents. Even when one did occur, it was solved amicably, not in the usual way, with a quarrel or a fight. Only one common enemy, the military dictatorship, brought such diverse peoples together.

Within our history, this is a rare moment of unity, discipline, determination and cooperation. How dare someone say that the people of Myanmar do not deserve democracy. How dare someone say that the people of Myanmar are violent, jealous and ignorant.

No sooner had some people noticed that some protestors couldn't afford to commute to protests in town centres than a free ride campaign was started. Some donors put currency notes for travel expenses inside free food packages. Cash envelopes were thrown into taxis carrying protestors. As soon as pro-military thugs smashed and destroyed protestors' cars, some workshops offered them free repairs and replacements.

When a military truck went into a poor neighbourhood and offered free rice to garner support, many people rejected the offer and banged pots and pans instead. But some wanted the free rice, complaining that they were poor. As soon as this was heard, a local store owner announced that those who needed quality rice could get it from her store free of charge. One woman in a village declared that all villagers could have free meals at her house until the junta gave up power on the condition that people join the protests.

Every night, the racket of banging pots and pans sound like war drums against the junta. While banging pots and pans, people also hurl curses at the junta and their associates, condemning them to failure and even death. Protests also happen as prayers. In many towns, people come together to pray for a better future or to spread metta to all corners of the cosmos.

To deter criminals and thugs, who were released from jail en masse in early February, and military and police agents, who are purportedly going round in town attempting to poison drinking water sources or engaging in arson attacks, people have formed vigilante teams to take care of their own neighbourhoods. These teams use smartphone apps to stay connected. After 1 am, when internet access is blocked by the regime, people distribute and use emergency numbers to report on suspicious things. Tech-savvy youngsters post video files, introducing apps like Brigefy, VPN, DNS and Zello to bypass internet problems and security.

From the very first day of the coup, it feels as though there has been no street-level government presence. People self-organise and mobilise their communities. The Committee Representing Pyidaungsu Hluttaw (the national assembly of elected representatives from the 2020 election) also asks that people form their own grassroots administrative units in order to defy junta-appointed village-level administrators. In many places, having met with alarming levels of resistance from locals, the junta's administrative staff have withdrawn from their posts.

Though thousands of civil servants have joined the Civil Disobedience Movement (CDM), some others remain in their jobs for the sake of the people. For example, local staff members of energy and electricity departments guarantee that there will be no electricity outages to households while thug attacks are on the rise and internet shutdowns are ongoing. Some municipal workers do their jobs as usual but don't wear their official uniform as they join the CDM. Medical professionals are the leading heroes of the CDM. It was them who started the campaign. They also help patients at free clinics. Not just government banks but also private banks are forced to close mainly due to the CDM. When the military bank Myawady re-opened after a week of protests, people formed long queues to withdraw all their savings. Within a week, it was closed again.

This is a new normal in Myanmar. It's not just small vendors that have refused to do business with police and soldiers. The number of restaurants and other enterprises who have joined the boycott against military-owned businesses is on the rise. The people of Myanmar have even boycotted the national lottery as it is owned by the military. The junta has announced that lottery winners will only be notified on 15 March, instead of the first day of the month as usual.

"Social punishments" are quick and effective. When the police opened fire at protesters in Naypydaw, and a 19-year-old girl was fatally shot in the head, people investigated the crime immediately. It didn't take long for them to disclose the culprit's name and rank, along with the names of his wife and family members and their businesses. This kind of public investigation is incredibly swift and results come in shocking detail. Activism that names and shames the oppressors is also a new normal for 'keyboard fighters'. Some police and military troops can now be seen disguised in full-length gowns.

On 24 February in Dawei, a town in southern Myanmar, police raided the house of a civil servant, a former military officer. The person had been supporting Aung San Suu Kyi and posted some protest messages on social media. A video record of the raid was shared widely on Facebook in which the son of the couple was heard defending his mother. His father was not home. He sounded like a kid no older than 7 or 8; only his voice could be heard in the video. He was courageously arguing with the police officer, saying, "You guys are not trustworthy." His words reflect people's feelings towards any member of the armed forces in the country, especially state police and the army. Even a child these days dares voice his opinion. This is also a new normal of the struggle.

On the other hand, life for dissenting writers, journalists and artists may be new but totally abnormal. A new amendment to the penal code related to high treason and other laws, such as privacy laws, has placed journalists under duress. Some news outlets have announced closures for a certain period. Some other news agencies, which are inclined to obey the junta, are put out of business as their employees walk out to join the CDM. The publishing industry has not been functioning properly since the beginning of February. With the CDM, no post offices are in service, no trains running, no banks operating and the distribution of books is simply impossible. Than Myint Aung, Maung Thar Cho, Min Htin Ko Ko Gyi, Htin Lin Oo, Saw Phoe Khwar and Lu Min were or are still under detention. We do not know their whereabouts. The group of early arrests comprises two writers, a film director, a pop star and an actor, respectively. Arrest warrants have been issued for all other artists and influencers who have actively endorsed the protests. They are now in hiding. Most of us cannot think of any near or distant future. All plans have been destroyed. No one is interested in anything other than the protests.

Despite the police brutality, people have been staging protests every single day since 7 February. During the first few days after the coup, the military organised pro-coup rallies. People waited them out until the thugs were no longer on the street to avoid clashes. Only on the evening of 5 February did a small group of people start off with a very brief protest in Sanchaung township in Yangon. The following day, four people held a longer protest in Mandalay. Three of them were arrested. And then, on 7 February, at least three hundred youths, led mainly by girls, started a protest in earnest. It spread like wildfire all over the country. Since then, protests haven't stopped, even on weekends. In some cities, prayer protests are held at night. As night falls, at 8 pm each day, the citizens of Myanmar take it as their duty to bang pots and pans against military tyranny. This is our unstoppable and persevering Spring Revolution.

At least fifteen people were killed by the end of February. The livelihood of thousands of civil servants is at great risk.

The livelihood of the general public is also uncertain. A tree is shaken up by a gust. Leaves fall prematurely. Nonetheless, who can stop the Spring, the Revolution?

Ma Thida, a native of Sanchaung, Yangon, is a surgeon, writer, former prisoner of conscience (from 1993 to 1999 at Insein Prison in Yangon) and Chair of PEN International's Writers in Prison Committee. As a dissident she has been a vocal critic of both the military regime and the opposition party National League for Democracy. She is now a research associate at Southeast Asia Studies Council at Yale University.

Nyi Pu Lay

from The dharma will prevail

[...]

THEN CAME 2020 and another round of elections. The NLD wanted to push forward with their agenda for the country's development. They wanted a landslide. Although their election campaign was stifled by COVID-19 restrictions, something special was in store for them. There were over five million youngsters who were voting for the first time.

Having come of age to vote for the first time, the young people wanted to vote for a party which they believed would bring about a federal union of their choosing. They counted down to election day in their calendars. They couldn't wait. Overseas voters had already cast their absentee ballots in advance. Some took leave from their job to travel to a ballot box. Many individuals travelled hundreds of miles by train, entailing several transfers, just to cast a vote in their home constituencies. Some travelled overnight to cast their votes.

In the countryside, people crossed mountains and rivers to vote. Some traversed orange orchards on the plateaus, others through tea plantations over the steppes, some took long motorboat journeys along the rivers, while others drove a three-wheeled htawlagi on a dirt road to go to the polls. After casting their votes, these men and women grinned, revealing their betel-blackened teeth, while some ethnic women danced, their huge silver earrings swinging with their moves, their belts adorned with silver coins clinking. Needless to say, they were overjoyed when the election result was announced, since it was a matter of life and death to them. The sounds of their spirited celebrations resonated across the sky. They thought casting a vote was worth it.

The mind that could think has cast a vote, thinking of the dharma. The heart that could feel has cast a vote, feeling for the truth. This vote would make our lives as humans worthwhile. We could live without fear. We would be able to breathe freely. Sound sleep would no longer be a dream. Our collective aspirations—rule of law, transparency, peace and democracy for more than fifty million people—appeared to promise a happy ending.

The military coup happened on 1 February 2021, just before the first parliamentary session was about to be convened. The president and the state counsellor were arrested. Union ministers were also arrested. The NLD was accused of electoral fraud. More than fifty million people collectively felt they had been duped.

The putsch was an affront to people everywhere. It was bullying by bullets. The plan to improve the 2008 constitution for a federal democratic union was ditched. People whose lives were already under the army's boots didn't take it lying down. Anti-coup protests erupted all over Myanmar. They were awe-inspiring. The protests happened as if people had coordinated a nationwide uprising. This wasn't the case. Their hearts simply responded to injustice spontaneously. Their minds decided to do what must be done for the country.

People protested in peace. They were disciplined. There were people of different ages, genders and ethnicities, mutually coexisting. They looked after one another. They helped each other out, for they knew they shared the same goals. They raised their hands in a three-finger salute and marched abreast. They came together and linked arms for a better future. They turned their backs to the COVID-19 virus after they became infected by the democracy virus.

Their leaders were born in the 21st century. Youths and teens who had hardly been out of their mothers' bosom. They were into computer games. They were into smartphones. They dropped all those luxuries to take to the streets. They protested peacefully. They were disciplined. Not a trace of garbage was seen in the aftermath of earlier protests in February. They yelled slogans. They sang protest songs in unison. They staged protests in front of foreign embassies. They demonstrated with various forms of artistic expression and performances. The world couldn't help but turn its head towards us. The protests by the Myanmar Generation Z became front-page news.

Then there was the CDM. "Stay home. Drive out of the dictatorship." The CDM was a strategic weapon that threw a spanner in the works of the junta. The protests and the strikes were effective. So the military beat and smashed the protesters with batons, threw tear bombs and stun bombs to disperse crowds. They would also use battle-grade grenades and live rounds. They employed snipers who shot innocent people in the head. Civil servants who were on strike were forcibly evicted from their homes if their homes were government properties. And yet the protesters' blood was red with courage. They were not to be cowed. Observers couldn't believe that the generation that was accustomed to K-pop and game apps had come up with several inventive forms of protest that had not been seen before.

Theirs was the fight between the dharma and ah-dharma, the tug of war between right and wrong, the arm-wrestling match between fresh imaginative minds and rotten kleptocrats. More than fifty million people against a band of armed men. A last-ditch fight.

Nyi Pu Lay (born 1952) hails from Ludu, a family of respected dissident writers, in Mandalay. He was a prisoner of conscience twice, in the late 1970s and in the 1990s. Best known for his short stories about down-and-outs, Nyi Pu Lay has published at least a dozen collections of selected short stories and three novels, and was honoured with a national literature award in 2016.

Dr Myint Zaw

from The noble

As THEY STAMP FORWARD, the black-hearted beat their batons against their riot shields, making frightening noises. They throw sound bombs to disperse crowds. They throw smoke grenades to darken every corner. A few days ago, there was music in those places. There were clamours: "We are youths. We have a future." [...]

The black-hearted pass real bullets into the hands of those who are armed with rubber bullets. The devil kneels, takes his aim carefully and shoots. Packed in the bullet that speeds out of the gun muzzle is grief. Grief for someone's children, someone's parents, someone's siblings. One thing we can say for sure—the bullet whizzes into an unarmed crowd. The place where the bullet ends its journey is where the grief begins.

There is also a scene at the place where the bullet begins its journey. When a bullet hits a target, the gunners celebrate. The video clips of such macabre celebrations will be seen by millions in disbelief in the years to come. A time will come when that very spot in the town of Dawei, where the gunners danced their celebratory dance, will be studied as one of the locations that witnessed the failure of humanity.

Human memory may be short, but the internet's memory is long. Do not expect the troops that are deployed in front of No. 5 State High School in Kamayut (Yangon), where Nyi Nyi Aung Htet Naing (1998–2021) was shot to death on 28 February, to be aware of this. Each day the troops will destroy tributes to Nyi Nyi, the bunches of flowers, wreaths, candles, photographs and other items that are placed in front of the school. Their destruction of memory will appear online within seconds. The internet will continue to document not just how Nyi Nyi has fallen, but also how his martyrdom has been destroyed each day.

The troops will certainly see Nyi Nyi's photographs as they destroy the tributes to him. What will the black-hearted think to themselves? Will they reflect in triumph, "How dare you challenge us?"

The black-hearted only bring ruin, deception and sadness. From Hitler to Pol Pot, there is more than enough evidence. The black-hearted look at the mound of broken bricks and boast that it's the golden palace they have built. "Are you as brave as us?" they ask, with assault rifles slung behind their backs.

The black-hearted always end up badly, because the noble have courage, beauty and wisdom. Strength cannot be found in apparently powerful black hearts. Those fallen over the past few days show the strength of the noble.

Someday in the future when people examine the heroes of Myanmar's Spring, they will see how the noble shine. Nyi Nyi, who was shot and wounded and carried off in a stretcher, raised his hand to show the three-finger symbol of defiance. Those three fingers have defeated the black-hearted.

"Everything will be OK" Kyal Sin's T-shirt reads. She must have chosen that T-shirt deliberately. Perhaps, at least for a moment, she must have thought about what she wanted to wear for that fateful occasion. The noble have no weapons. They only have informed choices, some of them may have been made on the spur of the moment. The noble are adorned with beauty and perfection. The black-hearted hate the noble for they have no such qualities. That's why they kick the noble with army boots. They beat them with batons. They shoot to kill. However, the thinking that they have prevailed each time someone is killed is beyond all reason.

When the black-hearted boast about their killing skills, the noble's message travels around the world. The message is written on Kyal Sin's T-shirt. The message is found in Nyi Nyi's three-finger salute. The message continues to travel far and wide. Never believe for a moment that the black-hearted have won.

Moe Way

The spirit

I sleep with
the spirit on my forehead.

Like a talisman
I would leave it at a high place
before I visit the loo.

The spirit
gets stopped and frisked in the house,
on the bus, and on the motorcycle.
It gets stopped and frisked
anywhere anytime.

Fallen heroes
may be lifeless.
They are not spiritless.
Their spirit is tattooed
on our skin.

When burned alive
the spirit sizzles and pops
like the flesh.

Like gemstones
the spirit outshines
the barricade bomb blasts.

The spirit body is the spirit.
The spirit breath is the spirit.
The spirit flag is the spirit.

Moe Way is a poet and a publisher who manages The Eras Books in Yangon.

Win Myint

Superfluities

"We need to pull back!"
Are you talking about my skin?
The way you grind your teeth
tells me you don't know
the difference between
shoulder and shoulder board.
In many forms of my human life
I have eaten
a lot of feet, fists and
fucks.
"You should put an antidote
in your poem," you say.
You must have been on ether
to repress memory.
Now you are blaming your age.
Behind me
there's no dagger.
There's just a door.
When you leave,
take your road with you.

First published in Burmese at moemaka.com, 8 April 2021. English translation in *Tripwire*, 18 September 2021.
Win Myint is a highly regarded contemporary Burmese poet and a builder who works in and around Yangon.

Nga Ba

Spring

Spring, seized,
turned into swallows.

Swallows, caged,
turned into clamours.

Clamours, silenced,
turned into scenery.

Scenery, covered up,
turned into eyes.

Eyes, forced shut,
turned into dreams.

Dreams, denied,
turned into maps.

Maps, destroyed,
turned into memories.

Memories, deleted,
turned into roads.

Roads, blockaded,
turned into ancillary legs.

Legs, smashed,
turned into wings.

Wings, clipped,
turned into breeze.

Breeze, detained,
turned into storm.

Storm, imprisoned,
spawned a million offspring.

Those offspring are our
inbreath & outbreath—

swallows in & out of
our nostrils—

our spring

Seng Bru

8 March

FOUR OF US FRIENDS joined the protests on 10 February. We, youths, gathered at and set out from Sitapur Manor field in Myitkyina, Kachin State. When we heard news that there were shootings and arrests in some other towns, one of my friends' mothers got very worried. We wore what we liked to take to the streets before. After she heard of shootings and arrests of protesters, she forbade us to wear black clothes. She must have been concerned that something untoward might happen to us if we wore black.

In the beginning of the protests we drank from purified water bottles supplied to us by well-wishers. Then there were rumours that bottled water was poisoned. No matter how thirsty we were, we no longer drank charity water distributed at protests.

As if a butcher were tearing a cow apart, police and army forces began to crack down on demonstrations in Myitkyina on 26 February. Tear gas grenades were thrown at the crowds on 27 February. On 1 March, they started to shoot with live rounds. Yet the youths of Myitkyina remained undeterred and continued to stage protests.

Once the army began to shoot with real bullets the number of protesters dwindled. However, some of us became more restless and continued to defy the dictatorial system. I remember the day when security forces started cracking down on us with tear gas—they chased after us like butchers after cattle, we had to head for the hills.

The army would snatch anyone who couldn't run fast enough. We had to outrun the soldiers to be free. We fled to safety so we could still take part in the protests the following day. When we ran we never looked back. We knew too well what could happen to us if we were caught. Sometimes we ran with concerns for those who couldn't run fast enough.

Some people were not tough enough. I felt bad about those who were left behind. I would like you to come visit this country so you can feel what I feel. When you are actually running for your life, lots of things are happening in your mind, but you can't tell what they are. Your heart misses many beats, not just because of the run, but because you are frightened you might get caught. During those nights, I thought of what happened during the day and couldn't sleep at all until the crack of dawn. Each time I heard a dog bark I would get up to the window to look out to the street in anxiety.

There is one day I will never forget. A sad day. It was 8 March. That morning when we, the town youths, came together at Awng Nan Catholic Church for a protest in downtown Myitkyina. The police came to arrest us. They parked their cars and prison vans at the entrance of the church and tried to enter the church to take us away. The priests reasoned with them and they didn't enter the church. When they left, we got a chance to get on with our downtown protest.

After the protest, on our way back to the church, we were confronted with brutal force by the police. We didn't realise military vehicles were hiding somewhere nearby. A young man and an old man were killed instantly by a sniper. They both were shot in the head. I was on the other side, so I didn't know what was going on. When I got back to the church, I saw people carrying the wounded on a stretcher into the church. The stretcher was drenched in blood. Everyone looked extremely sad. Someone said,

> "Soldiers are shooting at us from the top of a tall brick
> building. I didn't even realise someone had fallen next
> to me until people from behind shouted at me. I looked

back and saw him breathing with difficulty. I couldn't look at him anymore. I was overwhelmed. Thinking we could save him, we crawled on the ground to dodge bullets and pulled him back into the church while they kept shooting at us."

The young man they tried to rescue lost his life at the clinic near the church. Right before my eyes. He lost his life—he lost his soul. His body turned cold, he was dead. There was blood all over the clinic floor. That same day, I was told, there were some other patients who were shot in the stomach, but I didn't see them. In the church, people were strolling head down, with long faces. Some girls were extremely horrified. That day one of my friends from our group of four, who had been with us since the beginning of the protests, was arrested too.

I was in such a state that night. I kept having delusions that soldiers were coming for me. I couldn't focus on anything. There was an incessant ringing in my ears. I was hearing voices. The voices were loud and clear. They were the voices of resistance:

"Down with the military dictatorship! Our cause, our cause!"

"Democracy! Our cause, our cause!"

"Walk out of office. Break out of dictatorship!"

"If we retreat this time, we will have to live in defeat forever."

Seng Bru is a Kachin activist and a writer from Myitkyina, and founding editor of *Kachin Literary Magazine.*

Nhkum Lu

Sister Nu Tawng: Extraordinary courage out of everyday kindness

Extraordinary courage

SHE IS AN ORDINARY WOMAN, just like you and me. However, her selfless sacrifice and courage during one of the anti-coup protests in Myitkyina in February marked her out as a heroine for Myanmar and the world.

Her name is Sister Ann Rosa Nu Tawng, a Kachin Catholic nun, who was born in a small village in the northern Shan State, near China, as the fifth among thirteen siblings. I asked her why she decided to risk her life for others on that day. She said that she did what her heart told her to do and that it was the right thing to do at that moment. Let me tell you what happened on that day.

28 February 2021 was a Sunday. It started just like any other day for Sister Nu Tawng. She arrived early in the morning at the Mali Gindai clinic, where she still works as a medical lead. She monitored her patients to see if there were any emergency cases that needed immediate attention. Depending on the workload, she would sometimes start her day by cleaning the toilets, sweeping and mopping the floor, and taking the garbage out.

On that day, while she was checking on the patients as usual around noon, she saw a group of young people rushing into the clinic. They were asking her to save their souls, to let them hide inside the clinic. She thought she must get out of the clinic compound to see for herself what was going on out there.

On the street outside the clinic, she saw mayhem: a crowd of youths being chased by security forces. Their faces were pale with fright. Some were running and crying at the same time, some were screaming and a few of them had even passed out on the street. It was total chaos. She found herself in a war zone. People were being beaten up by the police, and gunshots were heard.

She was extremely shocked, but that didn't stop her from going towards the attackers so she could shield young people with her body and hands. She said to herself that she wouldn't run away. She felt she must protect and save her people. She couldn't care for herself, whether she would die or not.

In the thick of the police brutality, she cried and begged the security forces for mercy. She pleaded with them to let the young protesters go, as they were protesting peacefully. After a while, the situation calmed down, and the police and the protesters were separated. Then, she went in front of a policeman, kneeled down on the street and pleaded with him again not to beat the young protesters.

That scene, Sister Nu Tawng in her Catholic nun's habit on her knees with arms outstretched and facing a security personnel, was captured on the phone by a young protester and went viral. But that was not the end of the story.

On 8 March, Sister Nu Tawng found herself in the same situation again. When she heard noises from outside, she left what she was doing at the clinic to face the mayhem. This time she took cover behind a big tree at the corner of the street, silently stood there and observed what was happening.

When she saw a group of armed policemen charging towards the protesters she threw herself right in front of the policemen and kneeled before them, begging them not to hurt the young ones. She asked them to let the young protesters go home peacefully. Everyone was astonished to see Sister Nu Tawng in action again.

This time, she wasn't the only mediator. A Buddhist monk, inspired by her, showed up to lend support. The policemen, most of whom appeared to be Buddhists, were brought to their knees in front of the Buddhist monk and the Christian nun. They advised them to get out of their way. They were ordered to block the protesters by any means necessary, they said. Sister insisted that the police would only get to the protesters over her dead body. The police then ordered her to move and warned that her life would be in danger if she persisted. That afternoon, true to their words, the security forces shot at least two protesters dead.

Following that incident, Sister Nu Tawng was swamped with several interview requests from media agencies. The other nuns kindly warned her not to talk about her encounter with the police or any sensitive issues as they were afraid it might endanger her life. She told them not to worry about her. She urged them not to cry even if she died.

She wanted the world to know how the people, especially the ethnic Kachin in northern Myanmar, struggled for survival under the military regime and how hard life had been for them. She truly believed in telling the truth, even if the truth could cost her life. She said, "If I were afraid [of death], I would remain in the safety of my clinic. Why would I bother going outside to kneel in front of the police?"

Everyday kindness

Many people the world over found Sister Nu Tawng's courage on 28 February and 8 March extraordinary. I came to admire her even more when I got to know about her humanitarian work.

Within the first week of the coup, medical professionals in Myanmar launched the CDM and walked out of government hospitals. A shortage of hospitals meant that the Mali Gindai charity clinic was in a situation to accommodate a large number of patients on a daily basis, especially as there had been an increase in pregnant women giving birth.

The clinic, which is usually closed on Sundays, was now

open seven days a week. It was sought after by people who couldn't afford health care at private hospitals. Patients from all religious backgrounds and ethnic groups were welcome at the clinic. The clinic services were free for the needy, but it advised patients to contribute to maintenance, utilities and staff salaries as much as they could.

Sister Nu Tawng's very first experience of assisting in child delivery happened in the clinic on 9 March, when an evening prayer for the two young men who were shot dead in Myitkyina the previous day was held at the Catholic church. The mother-to-be arrived at the clinic that evening, and Sister made some arrangements for her before going back to her dorm.

At midnight, she received a phone call from the clinic that the woman's water had broken and that they needed her assistance with a normal delivery. There were police and soldiers on the streets, keeping an eye on the evening prayer.

Sister Nu Tawng made a detour, using the back door of her neighbour's to the clinic. She didn't even dare to use the torchlight on her phone. She was afraid that the police would notice her. She arrived at the clinic after much anxiety and difficulty, and successfully assisted the woman in labour.

The overstretched clinic was running out of beds. The woman she was assisting was in the bed where a young protester, who was shot in the head, passed away the previous day. In less than twenty-four hours or so, a newborn lay in exactly the same spot where a courageous young man had bid farewell to the world. "It was such a moment to meditate on our purpose in life, why we are here," Sister Nu Tawng mused. By the time she managed to wash her hands, it was too late to go back to the dorm. The police were still on the streets. She decided to stay overnight at the clinic.

Sister had been a nun for almost sixteen years by 2021. Humanitarian crises were not new to her. Her spirit of kindness grew in strength after she volunteered as a Cyclone Nargis relief worker in the Irrawaddy delta in 2008. Just three days after the Cyclone, Sister and her team were the first to arrive at one of the worst-hit areas in the delta. They were the first to help the locals whose lives and livelihoods had been wrecked by the tempest.

She remembered that there were scores of dead bodies floating in the tidal waters in the area. An estimated 100,000 people would have perished in the Cyclone. They made do with whatever they had to help the locals. At one point, they were short of clean clothes with which to wrap a newborn baby. Sister, with her white habit soaked in blood and sweat after a long day, demanded that a Catholic Father relinquish one of his longyis for the baby.

Sister had also been working with the internally displaced persons (IDPs) in Kachin State for many years. She had seen war children, victims of rape and sexual violence, and all other sorts of manmade trauma and tragedy associated with conflict. She saw the need to help the people with psycho-social support. Since the third wave of COVID-19 hit Myanmar in July 2021, she had been seen in personal protective equipment (PPE) on the front line on a daily basis at Mali Gindai.

"Difficulties and challenges notwithstanding, if we want to have this valuable thing that we call freedom, then we will have to work hard and sacrifice for it, even if it means dying, getting tortured or getting arrested. If we don't raise our voice now but hide […] just because we don't have the guts, we will have to go back to life as it was under the military regime. It would be like going backwards, and we would always remain oppressed," said Sister Nu Tawng.

I am convinced that many years of her selfless humanitarian work has made her who she is today, a strong and courageous nun, with a determination for public good. Here, I would like to pay my respect to each and every one who has taken part in the Spring Revolution of Myanmar. If you have been out on the street in the protests for freedom, you are a hero or heroine in my eyes.

We owe a debt of gratitude to other heroes and heroines of the Spring—from the street vendors who donated food and the people who handed out lunch boxes, water and juice bottles, and face coverings to young protesters to the people who showed support by clapping their hands when a rally passed by and the people who banged pots and pans in dissent.

Without each and every one of your support and participation, we could not have come this far in fighting for freedom in Myanmar. I hope we keep fighting for our freedom and raising our voices wherever we are. We can win in this fight. This is for us, the people of Myanmar, whether you are from a majority or a minority group. Let's keep raising the three-finger salute of resistance.

Nkhum Lu is a Kachin writer from Myityina. Before the 2021 Myanmar mayhem she was based in Yangon working for an international non-governmental organisation. She survived the third wave of COVID-19 which hit Myanmar in July 2021.

Ningja Khon

My story

The coup

IN THE FIRST WEEK of January 2021, in response to the word on the street about a looming coup in Myanmar, people began to mock the military chief Min Aung Hlaing on social media, with many girls posting, "Please seize me instead." In the run-up to the November 2020 election, we dreaded that the military might sabotage the whole election itself. No one took the rumours seriously in January anymore. Why would the military, which had more power than the civilian government constitutionally and in reality, need a putsch? After all, the military and their cronies had been enjoying numerous privileges, including the wealth they had amassed over the past 30 years.

As soon as I switched on my phone on the morning of 1 February, messages about the coup popped up in group chats. I couldn't believe my eyes. I immediately checked for reliable news. I heard that the Karen State minister had been apprehended in the middle of an interview with a Western media outlet. People who had been roundly ridiculed for reminding others that the military could come back to their previous position were now vindicated. For most of us, it took days to come to terms with the fact that the military generals had put an end to all kinds of development we, the numerous civil society actors and stakeholders, had built up over the past ten years.

I worked for an international non-governmental organisation (INGO). Security for our staff members and data became our top priority following the coup. We had to delete sensitive data from our personal computers and from our phones. All of a sudden keeping human rights reports became unsafe for all of us. Some documents were burnt. We took all necessary precautions such as installing a VPN (Virtual Private Network) on our devices and switching to more secure email clients and laptops. From mid-February, none of our staff members were allowed to use laptops or office computers. We relied on encrypted apps, such as Signal, for our communications.

After that, we were on a very important and risky mission to save Myanmar—we got in touch with protest leaders as well as members of the ousted parliament (Committee Representing Pyidaungsu Hluttaw, CRPH). Within days of the coup, we were providing financial and technical support to a plethora of protest groups across the country.

The protests

Having handed out a lot of cash to protest leaders in Yangon, I knew it would be unwise to go back to my flat. For a few weeks in February and early March I was given shelter at the houses of some former political prisoners in and around Yangon. I didn't stay at the same place for more than two consecutive nights. Later it got increasingly difficult to get around in Yangon. Sandbags and various other blockades appeared on the roads. Arson was commonplace. Getting a taxi was extremely difficult, even when one was prepared to pay an exorbitant price.

From sunrise to 11 pm, demonstrations raged on and on every single day from the second week of February, including the banging of pots and pans at 8 pm every night. I would usually participate in evening protests and sometimes daytime protests around Sule pagoda in downtown Yangon, along with hundreds of thousands of people. As I didn't have a car, getting around Yangon was very difficult. Once I spent the whole night at a guesthouse just to go to a place that is normally ninety minutes away. The sounds of gunshots from the military checkpoints were everywhere.

I had been sleeping in different places on the outskirts of Yangon for a couple weeks now. Sometimes I would have to go back to my flat on the sly. I was looking after a 6-year-old niece and a 10-year-old nephew, and they had been left in my sister's care. Whenever my sister had to go out for something, the children would be left alone, terrified by the sound of gunfire and explosions from the neighbourhood. My niece would call and ask me to come back. I couldn't resist her. I sometimes went back home to stay with the kids for a couple nights. The houses of some of my colleagues had been raided three or four times, but my flat was off the junta's radar since I no longer lived there.

The call

In the last week of February, acting on a tip from one of our partner organisations, I went to the office for the last time to collect all my personal belongings. I had a premonition that our office was endangered. I looked out from my office window for the last time. The view from my desk was still very pleasant; I could see a lake and a park. I liked my desk, especially in the monsoon season. It was nice to be at my desk, typing away on a long report, enjoying the sight and sound of the rain dripping down the large glass wall in front of me. After visiting the office, I went to stay at a different address for security reasons. I decided to get my waist-length hair cut. I had not been to a hairdresser since the COVID-19 restrictions were announced in Myanmar in March 2020.

One day, in the second week of March, when I was hiding in a Yangon suburb, a colleague called me on Signal. She had been out of touch for three or four days. All of us were worried about her. I was very happy to hear her voice. We were both chatting normally, until she began to ask some abnormal questions,

"Did you distribute the money you were supposed to?" I said, "Of course." Then she followed up with a question probing for details, "Your funds were this and that amount, right?"

I began to get suspicious. Why was she asking me questions she already knew the answers to? I had already submitted my report to the office finance team. After talking with her, I immediately reported to my team about our conversation. I alerted them that she might have been coerced to call me from a military interrogation centre.

Following that incident our office group chat was deleted. Now we were to communicate only with the security person assigned by the office. No individual staff member was allowed to call another on their own. The idea was that even if one of us were arrested, the junta would not be able to track us all down by following our communication chain. For about a month, I had no idea if any of my colleagues were safe. I could ask the security person, who was based abroad, about them, but they rarely gave me a full picture.

The raid

Our office was in a new high-rise in a business quarter in Yangon. It housed one of the first international retail shopping centres in Myanmar. We could get almost everything there: popular banks, retail shops carrying international brands, hypermarkets and department stores as well as local and international food and beverage outlets were all there. We shared the tenth floor with three other organisations, including a bank. The security at the building was very tight. CCTV cameras were everywhere. Visitors had to present their identity cards at the reception desk before entering the office building.

It was said that they raided our office at night on 10 March, a day or two after I received the dubious call from my colleague. When soldiers went to our office building, people suspected they were going up to the tenth floor to rob the bank. Security officers were forced to kneel down at gunpoint, their phones seized before they could report to anyone about the raid. The soldiers ordered that all CCTV cameras be turned off before they entered the office building. In an attempt to restore democracy in Myanmar, some of my colleagues worked relentlessly in our office until the night the office was raided. The military would search our office three more times afterward.

On 16 March, *Myanmar Radio and Television (MRTV)* announced that nine of our staff and two board members were on the list of arrest warrants on suspicion of lending financial support to anti-coup movements. The Burmese spelling of my name on the initial list was incorrect. When they made another announcement in April, they corrected the spelling. However, they still couldn't identify my hometown in Kachin state. They just put a Kachin township name as my hometown next to my name. I felt awkwardly relieved that they didn't get my details right.

The western border

Moving around from one house to another became increasingly difficult by day. After I got that call from my co-worker, I thought that the military might have already known my whereabouts. I began to look for a safer place. I heard some Western embassies had been helping some people since mid-February. As I had completed my MA in Canberra, the very first embassy I thought of was Australian. I called the embassy at least four or five times. Each time they said that they didn't have enough space and asked me to contact them later. I kept begging them to consider my case, but to no avail. When I reached the Australian embassy through an influential friend, they finally made it clear that they were unable to provide me with any sanctuary. My friend turned to the US embassy, which suggested I go to stay at their safe house outside Yangon. After a long journey, I arrived at the US embassy safe house, only to be told by the receptionist that the room was already taken.

A sense of despair kicked me in the head. I was carrying my travel bag, but I didn't know where to go. I tried to check in at some hotels in the area, but they asked me to present my identity card. I knew that the hotels were required to submit their guest lists to the authorities. Since I couldn't negotiate with any of the hotels, I walked around, my heart pounding heavily. Fortunately, I found a taxi and the driver suggested a hotel where his cousin worked as a receptionist. As soon as I checked into the hotel, I decided I had to use a new SIM card. I chewed the old SIM card and flushed it down the toilet. I switched to a Thai SIM card I got from one of the protest organisers in Yangon. Thai SIM cards were very popular; one could still access the internet with them even when the internet was blocked in Myanmar. We switched SIM cards at least every week. We knew the junta was twisting the arms of mobile telecommunication companies to use data spying software.

During those days on the run, my brain was on a 24-hour alert. It kept telling me how I should stay safe. I hadn't been able to sleep at night since mid-February. My brain was always asking what I would do if the door was kicked open by a squad of men. I would normally fall asleep around six in the morning only after I saw the sunrise. One night, I decided to flee to a remote area, somewhere I thought would be safer, somewhere I could stay for a long time.

During the third week of March, I took a bus to Kalay, a town near the Indian border in Chin State, western Myanmar, around 450 miles northwest of Yangon, that a friend suggested would be safer for me. In Kalay, I thought I would be able to cross the border easily if something happened. However, as soon as I arrived, there was intense civil unrest. To prevent military trucks from coming into the town, the townspeople had blockaded the main road with campfires and sandbags.

The soldiers cleared the blockades every morning but new blockades were erected by the people every night. During the nights, vigilante groups of young men would be doing rounds in their own wards. Dogs would be barking all night long and I still could not sleep. My ears became very sharp. I could hear as soon as the vigilantes started to walk around the street where I was staying. Where would I flee if the authorities came to check the household members list? I could hide at the construction site in the same compound. I could dislodge the temporary ladder after I got to the top floor of the building under construction. People would laugh at my super plan.

In Kalay, I put my cooking skills to good use. I would go to the market and prepare lunch and dinner for the host family. I didn't use my mobile phone or the internet. I didn't communicate with my office either. My friends were worried sick after they saw my name on the wanted list on state media. My mom couldn't call me directly. When I wanted to talk to my family, I used someone else's phone.

I was even thinking of changing my identity in Kalay. I asked someone who knew the immigration official there if I could use a Catholic name on my new identity card. The official, who seemed a very honest man, declined my request. Then I thought of changing my career. My mind was restless. Maybe I should start a small business? I was thinking of buying local produce in Kalay. Maybe I could sell them in attractive packaging in Yangon. I just wanted to keep busy with something I could focus my mind on. I wouldn't survive long without something to do. I went to the local market and checked what I could sell in Yangon. I took some pictures and asked my friends, who had a grocery shop in Australia, for some ideas. I was happy with my imaginary business, building a warehouse in Kalay where I could package food products.

By early April the anti-coup movement had escalated and

intensified all over Myanmar. In Kalay, locals had been fighting back with tumis or "handmade muskets". Demonstrators had been dying almost every day since March. On 7 April alone, the army killed eleven protestors and injured many others. Khu Khu, a woman activist from Women for Justice whom I knew was among the dead. I was about to go to her funeral, but her body was taken to another town.

On 9 April, an updated list of arrest warrants with our photos was announced on MRTV and in state-owned newspapers, which I learned from my office when I got back online. Friends had sent me the web links and photos of the news articles. A couple of days later, there were rumours that the military would be going door to door at night, searching for people like me. I was very concerned about my hosts. They too would be in trouble if I were found at their house. I had to move again. I gave up my budding business dream. At first I thought of crossing the border into India, but the Indian government's position on Myanmar put me off. I would go instead to the Thailand-Burma border. We had been working with some human rights groups in Thailand for years.

Travelling from Kalay to Yangon proved to be another challenge. Local resistance fighters, People's Defence Force (PDF), had destroyed bridges and in some places blockaded the roads with felled trees. One of the buses I was on got stuck in a river bank for many hours as the driver negotiated rough terrain and narrow cliff roads. Having to stop at numerous military checkpoints was even more terrifying. I wouldn't pray normally, but in those days, I prayed hard, especially near military checkpoints. God must have heard me. I arrived in Yangon safely.

The eastern border

As soon as I arrived in Yangon, I got in touch with my office security person. I sent a heads-up to my friends, who were based in a Thai border town, that I would soon be seeing them. I changed my hairstyle again.

On 11 April I set out from Yangon with a couple of activists for the eastern border in a bus. A few days before the mass shooting in Bago; at least sixty people had been reportedly killed but the actual death toll was believed to be much higher. The checkpoints were very strict—they rifled through everything we brought with us. I was travelling light, carrying a fake identity card, three dresses and some cash. They checked all our faces carefully against our identity cards, but the driver was known to the checkpoint authorities. They didn't ask too many questions when they heard we were going to Thailand for the Thingyan Buddhist New Year ("Songkran" in Thai), which was on 17 April. By sheer luck, we were able to cross all the checkpoints to Hpa-an, the capital of Karen State, about 100 miles southeast from Yangon.

Once in Hpa-an, we were picked up at the carpark of a shopping mall by an activist from a resistance group. As soon as he saw us, he reproached us for being in nice clothes. He wanted us to blend in with the locals. I was in a long-sleeve top. I wouldn't call it my most fashionable outfit. He remarked that my shirt didn't look local, as if I would know what was trendy for local girls. Then he kindly drove us safely to our lodging in a border town, where we were welcomed by a team of helpful activists.

We waited for a good day to cross the border. There were a few other activists waiting to cross the border like us. Our hosts suggested that we dress like local farm workers who would routinely cross the border to work as labourers in Thailand. I needed a worn-out dress. I picked a pair of oversized pyjamas

I found in a room, probably left behind by an activist. After three days waiting, we were dropped on the Moei riverbank on the Thai-Burma border. Two young men would lead us to the other side. All of our bags and belongings were left at the shelter. They only let us bring the most important items like cash and identity cards. I was in a pair of pyjamas, clutching a purse.

It was around 12 noon, lunch break for Thai border guards, the best time to cross the border. I was horrified as I learned we would have to walk across the river. I couldn't swim. The river seemed smooth and stable, but the water seemed pretty deep. Fortunately, a former political prisoner literally lent a hand. All the time, I was hanging on to his arm all the way across the river and never once did my feet touch the riverbed.

Once on the other side, we were totally soaked, but we still had miles to go. We walked across a sugarcane farm, a corn farm, many vegetable farms and several muddy ponds. We were behind the two young men, one of whom would usually check the route and give us an all-clear sign, telling us to step forward. When the guide said "Now run!" we ran. When he ordered "Now hide!" we hid. At one point we remained in a bush until he gave us an all-clear signal. I felt like I had turned into a proper refugee, but would I ever know the real flight of refugees from war and other conflicts? Some men in our group had to carry some labourer items as a disguise. A prominent human rights activist was carrying a bag of charcoal on his shoulders, and he was quite convincing.

I was just carrying a small shopping bag, but I got very tired and thirsty under the midday sun. I thought I'd like to take a rest in the shade of a tree. I wanted to go back home. I didn't want to run away like this. I didn't want to go anywhere. I felt like I had surrendered my pride and dignity. I was very embarrassed to be in pyjamas in front of strangers. I had never worn pyjamas outside my house in my life. I was also dead scared of being caught in ungainly pyjamas by the Thai border patrol. What if they took us into custody and took photos. I felt like it was a mistake to have come to Thailand. I hope no one saw, but I secretly wept.

After a long walk across the farms, we waited in a tent at a pickup point. An hour or so later the cars arrived. We jumped in and were rushed to Mae Sot, a Thai border town. That night was the very first night in a few months I managed to fall asleep. Still I woke up a few times during the night and reminded myself, "I am now in a safe place. No one would be knocking at the door. I can sleep without fear."

During those days I came across several very helpful and generous people. I will never forget their kindness as long as I live. I counted at least twenty-seven individuals and nine organisations which were involved in relocating us to Thailand. The individuals belonged to some human rights organisations and resistance groups. The people who had helped us cross the border were from local communities. The Thai intelligence services, our regional office, our security firm, and the US embassies in Thailand and Myanmar—they all must have coordinated our rescue. The UNHCR (the United Nations High Commissioner for Refugees) took care of us in Thailand.

The third country

By mid-May 2021, I was able to sleep well without having to remind myself of where I was during the night. A month later, with the help of my organisation and many others, I found myself in what the UNHCR called a "third country"—the United States (the second country being Thailand). I was given a one-year "parole visa". After one year, I could extend the visa for another year. We "parolees" were not given social security numbers and we could not work officially. Getting a bank account or a driver's license in the US was almost impossible.

My life now depended on the host community. People

brought me some rice, vegetables, meat and other necessary items. When I left Yangon I had over 1,000 USD with me. By the time I landed in the US, I had just 450 USD in my hands. I was in the care of different organisations and charitable individuals. Finally, after two months, my caseworker helped me open a bank account at a community bank. However, my bank doesn't link with any online banking services. I could only save and withdraw cash at the bank. Since I did not have a driving license, I had to depend on others to get around. I had always been an independent person and I wouldn't throw myself on someone's mercy. I felt very uncomfortable having to rely too much on others for basic items like food and my personal needs.

Even before the coup in Myanmar, imprisonment was not an option for me. I knew exactly what would happen to me in prison, as I used to work with former political prisoners, including female political prisoners, and learned their survival stories. I wasn't sure I would survive in a Myanmar jail. As long as I remained free, I thought I could still find ways to improve my country. After the coup I learned that, had I kept running inside the country, they would have caught up with me sooner or later. Besides, I would be endangering my hosts wherever I stayed. In the end I was convinced there was no place in Myanmar where I could feel mentally and physically safe.

The future?

Perhaps escaping from physical harm or persecution by fleeing one's country is the easy part. Will I ever escape from the mental trauma that's been with me ever since my first day on the run? Someone trolled me on Facebook, "From now on, you will only exist for your personal well-being. You are going to become a citizen there and live only for yourself, not for the community." And another, "Why did you have to flee. It was just a military coup [...] you didn't have to go that far." Those messages broke my heart.

Although I am safe now, I am not as happy as I was before February 2021. I am not as active as I used to be. I sleep my days and nights away. Sometimes I binge on films. I've lost interest in news; video clips of people in distress trigger my anxiety. I avoid things that I normally enjoyed doing. I tend to get easily irritated. My memory usually returns to the flat I bought, my room, my desk, my books that I have not finished reading, my mom, my family, my talkative niece, my friends, my clothes, my cosmetics, my traditional Kachin dress, the restaurant that I normally ordered food— all the things I love are gone now. I have to build a new status, a new job, and a new credit history to prove that I am a good citizen in the US.

Some people suggest I work at an Amazon warehouse. What am I supposed to do at an Amazon warehouse? I don't see how my past experiences are relevant for Amazon. I had worked for a better, a more equitable society in Myanmar. I would have to work for the world's richest man if I chose Amazon. My former office continues to support me with everything, from dealing with complicated legal documents to my personal finances. I don't feel right about it either. I find my uncertain status on a parole visa the most disturbing. Now I can imagine the life of an undocumented immigrant. What about Rohingya people who have been fighting for their legal status in Myanmar and some other countries?

For now I simply don't know how to manage my mental health. Someone suggested I talk to a mental health counsellor to relieve the stress and negative thoughts associated with survivor's guilt.

My hosts here assured me, "Now you can start a new life. You know English and you have had a good education. You will be fine after a while."

And yet I am still undecided whether I should trade my ideals for my survival in the US. Perhaps it is okay to feel guilt. I believe my energy will return sooner or later. When I get my energy back I will definitely be back on track—for my people.

Ningja Khon was a program officer at a human rights organisation in Yangon in 2021. She had previously worked as coordinator for Kachin Women Peace Network in Myanmar and, prior to that, coordinator for Kachin Women Association Thailand, among others. She holds a Master's degree in International Relations from the Australian National University (ANU).

Pandora

John, I am drifting along the River Burgundy – 3

John, they say, life is short.
What a tall thing the Revolution is!
Is that normal?
Old normal, or new normal?
Abnormal normal?
Over here there's no more sundown breeze.
All lights are put out before the sunset.
We look forward to the sunrise in the east.
Shall the sun ever rise again?
Radios are making a comeback.
Don't you post not-so-newsworthy virus news.
In these troubled times,
even lovers make do with guerrilla kisses.
How youthful their burgundy bloods are!
A glass of Burgundy red, to go with a piece of red meat?
By the way, do you still read like ah…ah…ah?
There's nothing you dare not do, John.
Do you dare die?
The world seems to be in a big shock,
because we dare live.
Nursing a sneaking envy for the dead, we learned
to distinguish between a sound bomb and a musket.
A fart and a wet fart are different too.
Have your foe and your self been divorced?
Here's a riddle for you—

Not an anyein-pwe, zat-pwe or a feast.
What do you call a fiesta that has no fun whatsoever?
Don't say sit-pwe for war, or tike-pwe for battle.
Sometimes the pebbles thrown at you from behind
hurt more than the bullets in your chest.
"Aren't American troops being pulled out?",
the email from Kabul asks. "I think your cities haven't
seen real war. In Afghanistan we are used to
real war in our forty years of nonstop sit-pwe."
By the way, do you still read like, wah… wah… wah?
If there's such a thing as inauthentic war
we'd add that into our bar snacks.
Sovereign affairs are as subtle as the colours
of chicken eggs, as delightful as mountains of clouds.
O … in an infinite universe of infinite choices,
K Zaw's poem goes, we have had to resort to the dharma.
I have convinced myself,
all of this must be a nightmare.
In my nightmare, I was lining up at the ATM, and
the bank collapsed. I forgot how to run.
The River Burgundy turned out to be
the River of Poets' Blood.
Some people sobbed, reading poetry.
"You guys are pathetic softies!",
I gave them a teary nag.
John,
schools will reopen soon.
Will the windows of education ever open again?
The hands that should hold books hold guns.
Stethoscope hands, makeup artist hands,
fine artist hands, sickle hands, et cetera, et cetera.
Look John,

for tools to go back to their rightful hands,
for us to reclaim
our sleep, our smiles,
our families, our free times,
our own lives, our sundown breeze, and
the souls of those who dared to sacrifice
from kleptomaniacs
we are trying with our bare hands
that have been dropped by diplomats.
Day in day out
we crawl with these bare hands.

The poem is dated 14 May 2021. First published in Burmese at moemaka.com

Pandora is a Burmese poet, essayist and blogger. She has published two anthologies of Burmese women poetry, the first of their kind, in Myanmar. Just before the military takeover in 2021 she received a national literature award for poetry in "transitional Myanmar".

Poet of No Identity

Drone paints

moon flowers. moon birds. flower moons. high mountains. chains. changes. love. dwarfs. reds. whites. blacks. greens. garden of innocence truths hidden in the runnels of running fire. irons. steels. air balloons. vision. enthusiasms.

"Success is moving from failure to failure without losing enthusiasm." winston churchill. questions. books. meals. births. kindness. vows. youths.

life is still beautiful early in the mornings through the window reaching up the green garden. humanity dreams.

drone carrying authentic possiblity-impossibility realms of brainy lives in the stream of poetic singularities.

springs

Nandar

A nightmare you can't wake up from

I WAS BORN in a traditional Nepali household in a Shan State village in the north of Myanmar, where "because you are a girl" is the reason to do or not to do something.

"Why do I have to help in the kitchen?" Because you are a girl. "Why can't I play with boy friends?" Because you are a girl.

So, I grew up with a lot of unanswered questions in my head, such as, why don't my brothers do their dishes? Why can't I visit temples during my period? And why can't I go out after 6 pm?

Like many teenage girls in my village, I had a goal to one day get married, have children and take care of my husband.

I heard somewhere that when you put a fish into a tank, it can only grow up to the size to fit into the tank but if you put it into the ocean, it will freely grow as much as it naturally does. I think it is the same with our brains.

Our brain is like a fish. If we live in a narrow-minded society where girls and boys are put into a box, we will think inside the box to try to fit in. Like the fish in the tank, I was trying to fit into the society I was raised in. I did all the things that are required to be a good girl, even though they were making me deeply unhappy.

I got a scholarship in 2014 that changed my life and my goals. In this social science programme, I learned for the first time that what we are socially conditioned to believe is not the only way to lead our lives. And that, as humans, we are born with rights that nobody—not the government, not even your family—can take away from you. My path to understanding my rights led me to activism.

It started when I stood up for myself and my rights to my family. I truly believe that just like violence begins at home, justice must also start from home. It was a long, ugly, slow process of making them trust me and my capacity to lead my life without their constant distrust or judgment over my gender.

I began my path to achieve financial independence by working in a local NGO as a teacher.

It felt like what Gloria Steinem meant when she wrote that "\$50 that you earned gives you more strength than \$500 that others give you."

In 2017, after translating and publishing *We Should All Be Feminists* by Chimamanda Ngozi Adichie, my career took a turn from being a teacher to being a full-time activist. Through my writing and speaking, I actively became outspoken about the gender issues and cultural violence that women and girls have to face in my community.

Even though I had earned trust and support from my family, I started receiving harsh judgment and exclusion from my community. Many of them called me a "cultural ruiner" because I was challenging the harmful practice in the Nepali community in which menstruating girls are banned from their houses and prohibited to touch anything or go anywhere.

We call women who are bleeding "nah chu ne"—the literal translation is "untouchable". Our society fails to see this as a problem because their brains are like the fish in the tank. They do not get to grow.

With the help of the internet and the slow steps towards democracy, I was able to extend my work internationally by starting the Purple Feminists Group in 2018 to raise awareness about gender inequality in Myanmar.

I was also able to provide educational training and workshops to university students, teachers, government workers, doctors, lawyers and religious leaders to think critically about gender issues. Along with that, I ran two feminist podcasts with my team to amplify women's and girls' voices on topics including abortions, toxic relationships, menstruation, politics, domestic violence and more.

Then, right when we were starting to see a gradual but growing interest in feminist topics by the people of Myanmar, the coup occurred.

On 1 February I woke up with no cell signal and quickly realised that something terrible had happened. I looked out into the street and saw many people were running and panic-buying. I needed some confirmation that what I thought happened had happened. I could not check the internet or call anyone to ask. I kept looking outside to get an answer, and saw military trucks playing the national anthem loudly and proudly to declare their success.

I felt devastated, angry, sad, helpless and hopeless, and I froze. Those feelings are complex and hard to process.

From that day, curfews were announced, fears were reinstalled, connections were cut, lives were lost and hope was diminished. That day can be marked as the beginning of living with the familiar fear with which our parents had lived.

As a feminist advocate who has been working in advancing the women's rights movement for years, it felt like the progress we had made collectively had just evaporated. I felt extremely unmotivated to do any work. It felt pointless and meaningless to be doing anything about gender equity if the dictators were going to rule the country. And, realistically, if we continue doing it inside Myanmar, our lives will be taken away. So, I paused all the work that I was doing—producing the podcast, creating content and providing training.

I started joining the protests every day to show solidarity and because it was the only way to fuel our hope. By showing up to the protests, by standing up for each other, by rejecting the coup, we hope that we will one day get what we deserve— justice and equality.

Being disconnected from the world overnight is such a scary thing—especially when you have been connected for so long. The experience of living under the coup is like a nightmare that you cannot wake up from. It is like a storm that never stops. It is like an earthquake that destroys everything.

I returned to Yangon from Shan to work on relocating out of Myanmar. On my way back, the highway roads were filled with police and the military intimidating civilians. "Are you joining the civil disobedience movement?" "Are you doing anything illegal?"

What was more startling for me was to witness the sad, quiet, damaged Yangon. Yangon used to be a lively, fun and extremely busy city, especially at night. But now I see very few people walking outside, even in the daytime. There are no loudspeakers, there is no music, no business, no smiling, no crying—just complete darkness with lost lives and unheard voices.

Following the coup, Myanmar has become a country that is hard to recognise as it used to be—peaceful and lively, yet complex, hardworking and beautiful.

We have lost more than a thousand lives and there has been immeasurable suffering, yet we don't give up. The people who gave their lives for this aren't simply numbers.

Their lost lives will become scratches on the wall as proof that we fought, and are still fighting, back. The scratches will keep us and our voices alive even if we die.

First published in *Index on Censorship* Vol. 59, No. 2, Summer 2021.
Nandar is a women's rights activist. She has fled Myanmar after writing this piece but is safe and well in another country.

Khin CM Maung

In the shadows of tyrants

1994—I was born under the shadow of the previous military regime. For children of that time, joy was a privilege negotiated under our parents' protection. How much they could shield us from reality dictated our lives. In that afforded ignorance of youth, we found happiness even under a dictatorship. I remember it vividly, lining up for rations with my mother, the small bag of gritty brownish sugar slipping between my fingers like sand in an hourglass. The small booklet she kept tucked in her pocketbook, how the lady at the counter stamped that book so rudely every time. But children chuckle and smirk in the night lit by the candles melted onto the bottom of old condensed milk tins. When the electricity was turned back on, we would cheer and clap. Cloaked under mosquito nets on summer nights, we slept well as our aunties fanned our bottoms with old newspapers. It was a way of life that was beaten into this sunken earth we call Myanmar.

It was a time when a portrait of General Than Shwe would hang in the offices of every business, ministry, school, and hospital, much like an unholy saint glaring behind his gold frame glasses. My father, who was born in 1961, also grew up under this same shadow—his saint was General Nay Win. For those of us who have grown up living under the watchful eyes of the Tatmadaw, we know life is unfair; we know it is unpredictable; we know what is taken from us was never ours to begin with; and we understand that some things, some unfortunate events, must be left alone—whether just or unjust. This was the life we were ordained into, an honorable suffering under the Buddhist way of life. All questions seemed to be answered by Karma—by

"If it is, then it must be." How can we know what we did in our past lives to have earned such suffering? Who could say? But on the Karmic vehicle of Myanmar, the driver never seemed to have bad Karma of his own.

*

Sanctity and sanity were broadcast every 8 am and 8 pm over the radio and the television. The news every night showed men in green uniform cutting ribbons, planting trees, praying at holy sites, and raising pagodas. The ladies on the state channel, Myawaddy, were always thoroughly kempt, their clothes perfectly tailored to their bodies, their hair so tightly sewn into a bun that the edges of their faces pulled their brows back into frozen, shocked expressions. The men were stocky and black-browed, dressed in starchy white shirts and pasoes. The women fair-skinned, the men just tan enough to be Bamar and nothing else. Every night they swayed, shawls waving left and right, clapping in unison to tunes touting propaganda. For the longest time it felt like that's all we watched, their bodies dancing their audience into a trance.

2001—the first time I watched an anyeint, traditional Burmese entertainment that combines dance, music and comedy routines, on video. The troupe had five men with thick oily hair, their outfits haphazardly put together. Their pasoes merely tucked together, sweat soaking gray spots on their white shirts. The footlights on the stage made them sweat beads as they performed skits. The one who stood in the middle was the ringleader, the stooge. The short one to his left was his funny man, the tall one was the fool, the two others were his sidekicks. One sillier than the next, the stooge could never keep up with their foolery. Occasionally the tape would skip, and I would hold my breath hoping to catch the punch line. And there were occasions where the tape would skip, but only to return to the sound of hooting and hollering from the audience.

"What happened to the tape?"

"They cut the joke."

"What happened to that part?"

"It probably didn't make it past censorship; we can still watch the rest."

"What didn't pass censorship?"

Usually, no one answered this question. In their mind I was probably too young to understand, and too dangerous for an undisciplined mouth to carry such sensitive information around in the schoolyard. It was not long before I understood the gags—the sly comments on electricity and water shortages, poverty, the military nepotism, the shadowy figure they called "Ah Ba"—Burmese for father or godfather.

The stooge would muffle the fool before he could even blurt the political punch line. His eyes wide in comical fear, shushing his audience not to laugh at the obvious. We all existed under those omnipresent eyes behind gold rim spectacles. If we were all to laugh freely at our oppressors, they would surely be the only ones left to live in their fool's paradise. Nonetheless, there was always the tinge of anxiety that they would know we laughed. If the evening breeze would betray us and carry our laughter to the police station; if they could hear our forbidden merriment emitted through our open windows; if they learned that in our minds, we knew that this was a fool's paradise and that they indeed were the fools, what would happen to us?

But we laughed, gasping for air at the stooge's gaping fear, his shushing finger.

We laughed.

*

2014—excited citizens stood on Shwegondaing Road staring at the bright LED screen mounted on the side of the National

League for Democracy (NLD) building. The ticker at the bottom of the screen flashed red and white every ten to fifteen minutes for the clamouring crowd. The by-election results were being announced that evening and people came in droves to watch the results announced in front of the Yangon NLD office. Some spectators squatted on a distant curbside, while others maneuvered their way into the front of the packed road. Children sat on their fathers' shoulders clapping and cheering with the crowd, their faces lit red by the LED that flashed above them.

My aunty and I parked at the intersection and walked to the rally. One could hear the crowd from each end of the street, singing songs of democracy and freedom. With each flash of the LED screen there was a burst of applause; the excitement in the air was palpable. It was the sound of the people's thirst quenched. The voices reverberated that evening, a prophecy unfolding on an ordinary street, on an ordinary humid Yangon evening. And we, ordinary citizens, watched the end of an era illuminate off the side of a building as we braced to welcome the start of another.

*

My father and I have been lucky to vote a total of two times in our lives; my grandmother, who is currently 98, has been fortunate to have seen five elections her entire life. That day was an occasion. We woke early to make it to the polling stations. The lines were long, but people waited with patient anticipation, eager to dip their small finger into that distinct pot of blue dye. At the gates of the polling station people stopped to take selfies, photos of their dye-dipped pinkies, a snapshot of the day's fate was seized by 23 million pinky fingers. The votes we cast in 2015 and 2020 were bought with the lives of those who died for the cause of democracy, those who have sacrificed everything, including their families.

Soon, they took down General Than Shwe's photo from my father's office. First no one had the nerve to do it. It seemed ungodly, cursed, to even think of removing it. But day by day surely that fear faded. The photo was removed, but kept in the backroom, just in case. Before 2015 we had survived, but had not yet lived. In the early years of the democratic transition, there were shadows of doubt, but what lingered more heavily were the fears we had grown accustomed to living with—the fear to speak, the fear to act, the fear to want more than we were allowed. But the more freedoms we were allowed, the more we believed, the more we dared to hope that all people would have an equal position in society, access to better healthcare, opportunities to make a living, and the dignity to live their life as they chose.

Our democracy is not perfect. It is fragile as any democracy is. There have been injustices, untruths and unfulfilled promises, for which there are no excuses to be made. But I write as someone who comes from a country that has been broken down generation after generation, someone who has learned to live in fear for nearly four generations. A democracy, mighty or meagre, is an opportunity to live a life free from oppression.

I write this now, many months into the 2021 coup—many lives stolen, freedoms lost, old fears reawakened. The people of Myanmar and its diaspora are still resisting. We will persist as we did in our youth, to find small pockets of happiness amid crisis, because we are human. We, too, lay our heads down to sleep, eager to wake in the morning. We, too, work to feed our families. We, too, have felt the light of freedom in our lives. When you hear our stories, take heed, and remember the fragility of life. I ask you to defend the democracy of your country and every country around the world, for tyranny needs no companions.

Thett Su San

Teacher X

ONE EVENING, while giving a lower body massage to my octogenarian mother, I glanced at the sky through the window beside her bed. It was red, an unusual colour, as if the heavens were very upset. I recalled what Mother used to tell me about the red sky when I was a child. A bad omen! A country could be in great peril if the sky over it turned red! From time to time the sky over my hometown in Mandalay would be red, and I no longer thought anything special of it.

*

In 1996, I was in my early 20s when I became a state school teacher. I was posted to a primary school in a village in Nawnghkio, a laidback rural township in northern Shan State. The country then was under The State Law and Order Restoration Council (SLORC), led by Senior General Than Shwe. There weren't enough teaching aids or materials at the village school. Most ethnic people in the area had never been to school, and they didn't think much of their children's education either. It was down to us teachers to convince both the parents and children about the potential benefits and values of public education.

The salary was barely enough for me to survive, let alone support my parents. I couldn't even afford to pay regular visits to them in Mandalay, about 100 miles south of Nawnghkio. Even after three years in Nawnghkio, my name was not on the list of transferred teachers.

In 2000, Father visited me with some good news. I was

going to move back to my hometown. There wasn't any public transport to the remote village where I worked, and yet Father managed to come see me all by himself. I couldn't give him any money when he left. Watching the bullock cart Father was in squeaking out of my sight, I realised how much I missed home.

Before Father's visit, a friend and I applied for a university tutor position. We had to take written and verbal tests. We both passed the written. During the verbal, the officer blatantly demanded 2,000,000 kyat in cash. One of the requirements to pass the test, he added. I earned only 2,000 kyat per month at that time. 20 lakh was a lot of money. With a little help from her well-to-do family, my friend got through the test and landed the job.

The first four or five years at my new school in Mandalay weren't easy. In Nawngkhio, teachers were passionate about education. Teachers and students were like a family. We created teaching aids ourselves. But I experienced culture shock at my new school in Mandalay. The teachers there didn't take teaching seriously. They didn't care about students' progress in the class. They ran private classes or "tuitions" only a few parents could afford. At school, they favoured their own tuition students. To my surprise, many parents trusted them. Initially, they didn't trust me, someone with a few years experience at a rural school. Many of those tuition students ended up in my class after their final exams. Some students, including those who made top grades, turned out to be below average. It took years for me to accept the fact that a school teacher's salary was not enough in a city like Mandalay. I became one of "them", a tuition teacher for children in my neighbourhood. Still, I wouldn't give private tuition classes to students from my own school.

When the National League for Democracy (NLD) won the 2015 election, the whole country seemed to be on cloud nine. We thought the light of justice was about to break through the darkness of the military era. We would enjoy the fruits of our hard work. We would be fed well and kept warm under a blanket of freedom. As a member of the education department, I was proud to be part of a collective effort to catch up with the rest of the world in basic education over the following five years.

*

That evening, while kneading Mother's legs, I thought to myself, "What would I want more in this life? What a blessing it is for me to be able to look after my bedridden mother, to be able to teach children, to know right from wrong, to live in a democratic society." The following morning when I was getting ready for the wet market, I heard terrible news. There was a military coup! I thought I was going to suffocate, or my head was going to explode. I almost screamed at the top of my lungs.

The atmosphere was filled with anguish. We didn't believe the news at first. My brother called a cousin and confirmed, "It is true! Daw Aung San Suu Kyi has been detained!" We sat in total silence, dismay and denial that whole day. At moments like these, one wished one were a superhero. For days to come I continued to feel hopeless and hapless.

On the third day after the coup, I heard healthcare workers had launched the CDM. Some people had taken to the streets. I thought that education staff should be on strike as well. On the morning of 6 February, an anti-coup rally of thousands of motorcycles took place in Mandalay. The following days, bank employees, railway workers, lawyers, firefighters and civilians walked out. At the time, I was taking care of Mother and Sister, who were both unwell.

From 16 February, I joined the protests with some of my colleagues from my school. Seeing thousands of people giving three-finger salutes in unison in defiance of the junta uplifted my mood. I felt I was doing a very important job for my people and country. Our revolution would succeed, I was convinced.

Along the thoroughfares in Mandalay, many stalls popped up, handing out food packages and beverages to protesters. The sight was overwhelming. That kind of charity happened every single day since the protests began, a friend said. It was incredible to see how passionate our people felt about freedom and how generous and supportive we were of each other in a crisis like this.

The days when I was part of sit-in protests in three places—in front of a local police station, near Zegyo Market, and on 62nd Street—were nerve-wracking. Frightened of getting shot or arrested, I was always working out possible escape routes in my head. I had bad knees. I'd better be well prepared, I thought.

On other days I would simply join the crowd on the sidewalk in support of protest marches. Hundreds of marchers came and went, and with them the distinct attire or uniforms of diverse ethnic groups, led by religious leaders. We all took to the streets for one reason—to overthrow the military regime and restore democracy.

As the days went on, the junta's violent crackdown became more widespread. Some people appeared to be putting on brave faces, but their eyes told me they were exhausted and shattered. Most of the people who took to the streets and fought and died for the country were unknown civilians. Some of their names we learned only after they were shot to death. Some celebrities and social media influencers who were holier than thou in the early days of the Spring Revolution disappeared once the violence began. Some of them had been detained, but others just chickened out.

This whole thing was wrong. I felt increasingly bitter again with each passing day. I couldn't hold back my tears. I thought my life as a primary school teacher for twenty-five years had been unjustifiably bad. Millions of my compatriots were in the same situation—or even worse! Who will benefit in the end: the military top brass and their families, their cronies, and influencers who were holier than thou again? I began to wonder.

*

In 1987 I was a fresher at Mandalay University. We had a relatively decent education. After the 1988 uprising, the military-controlled education system deteriorated. Libraries were empty, and universities were opened for months and shut for years. Our lecturers would hand out papers to learn by heart for the exams. Lengthy closures of universities by the SLORC, in fear of student uprisings, meant that it took seven years for me to collect a BA certificate.

To make matters worse, the junta kept experimenting with new curricula in all sorts of schools in the 1990s. They replaced the quasi-socialist agenda in the textbooks with a pro-junta patriotic one. Whenever an education minister or other officials would come to inspect our school, we would always be given advance notice. There was no such thing as a spot check. The quality of teaching, students' progress and behaviour in school, and how teachers should be promoted based on their merits were never investigated. They merely checked school records. It was only after 2015, under the NLD government, that refresher courses for school teachers were given during summer holidays. Those courses I found very valuable not only for me, but for the general improvement of the quality of basic education in the country.

*

Just when I thought my country was heading in the right direction, the military dragged her down the drain again. Just like in the SLORC era, we now have to put up with the state-owned Myawaddy and *Myanmar Radio and Television* propaganda. I miss my late father whose ears were always glued to his shortwave radio for independent broadcasts from abroad in the SLORC era. Father was one of those lucky ones perhaps. He died of old age peacefully, just before the double carnage of COVID-19 and Coup-21. He would be turning in his grave if he knew that even a shortwave radio had become illegal in 2021.

Today millions of unknown civilians continue to defy the junta in their own ways. I participated in the CDM and decided to give up my cherished job after twenty-five years. I will never return to the position of a state school teacher as long as the military regime is in power. Some people have lost their lives, limbs or loved ones. Giving up a livelihood is the least I should do.

This essay was written based on an anonymous first-hand account that was told to the author.

A Phaw Khaing

For my martyred son

Here lies
Min Khant Soe, my son!
Holding the law of death
he has sculpted history.

Chronicles are written
in blood that's shed
in Okkala.

O my beloved son,
my son,
the flower in full bloom
has fallen off before its time.
With what grief
I will grieve for you!

Rest in peace, son!
Write democracy in gore.
Look
there are fallen flowerets like you,
all red on the asphalt road
singing the song of peace.

Min Khant Soe was shot to death in a protest on 14 March 2021 in front
of Children Hospital in North Okkala.

Zaw Lu Sane

We call it the North Beach

With I-don't-give-a-fuck
attitude from 1988, I too lifted
my paso & flashed my cock at
those motherfuckers.

No negotiation between
guns & roses,
the North Beach wrote this in blood.

Corpses have been found floating
in the water spinach farm before.
In the town square today
the fallen are found adrift.

In the place, where
a granite obelisk for martyrs was dug out
a granite mountain will rise.

The military hounds have sharpened
their fangs at the North Beach.
They have chosen
the North Beach to hone their bullets.
We, we will sharpen our revolution
against their throats.

The North Beach,
we call it the North Beach!

The scent of your fallen flowers,
extraordinarily sweet.

"The North Beach" is slang for North Okkalapa, an impoverished township in Yangon, which was brutally attacked by security forces and scores of protesters died in March 2021. At least 20 people were reportedly killed on 3 March 2021 alone.

Thitsar Ni

Hlaingthaya

Up against the metropolitan Yangon
Hlaingthaya is wilderness,
for apoetical Tarzans.
This is where the Irrawaddy delta hobos,
who didn't witness the World Wars
but pushed through the Cyclone Nargis, and the Anyar Mongols,
who left their farms for factories, mingle.
Myanmar's New England doesn't reek of butter.
They don't need a five-star hotel here.
There's Mee-kwet wet market for vegetables.
The place is as plain as instant tea without cream.
The durian husk is known for spikes,
the township is known for hooligans.
At times, it will wash its misdeeds down
in labour protests.
On the Hlaingthaya special menu are
slums and sweat beads,
meagre meals and moonshine stench,
factory smoke and melees.
Those who are squeamish about mud
wouldn't set foot here.
And yet Angelina Jolie has been here.
Aung San Suu Kyi has been here.
In the Spring Revolution
women of this town get obscene at the Senior General,
men brandish sticks and dahs,
children and grown-ups come together,

"Repress us, we will rise again.
Touch us, we will strike back!"
The curtain to the first defensive war is lifted.
The ideology of the people who haven't got
their nose into "surplus value theory" is
we-have-nothin'-to-lose-ism;
they spit it out like quid betel.
Had only a superior power prevailed
David would have never beaten Goliath.
A revolution without the precariat is a wingless bird.
A poster reads, "If I am cut down,
the man behind me will cut you down."
Black flags have been raised
on the side of righteousness.
In this sapped spring of endless legends
they will thrive like a flower jungle.
Death is no stranger—
if you daren't fall, you are no flower.

On 14 March 2021, at least 39 people were reportedly killed in the protests in Hlaingthaya township at the outskirts of Yangon.

Thitsar Ni

from Mindat

The renown of the town
the size of a banyan seed has grown
as big as a giant banyan tree.
In news after news, come laurels
after laurels for Mindat from Chin State.
Wearing the Chin Hills around her neck
the faithful hornbill branded the word Mindat
right on the forehead of the Spring.
Mindat, a town at an altitude, where
clouds and houses become indistinguishable!
True to your own history, you say,
"A true 'Salai' will always carry
a palaing basket and a dah with him."
Mountains are your boots, gorges your mattress.
The tumi musket in your hands
turned into a wand against the devil itself.
Hear, hear the battle gong from a town
4,000 feet above the sea level!

Hornbills and Taungzalat (rhododendron flowers) are the symbols of the Chin Hills at Myanmar-India border. "Salai" denotes courage and is a common honorary prefix to Chin men names. "Palaing" is a type of bamboo wicker basket commonly used all over Myanmar.

Fighting erupted in Mindat, in the southern Chin state of western Myanmar, on 24 April 2021 after the military refused to release seven detained youths. By August 2021, more than 80 ethnic Chin people were reportedly killed in Chin State.

Thitsar Ni (born 1946) has published more than thirty books, from poems, essays, short stories and literary critiques to science fictions and religious and philosophical treatises, including a dictionary of world politics. Thitsar Ni is a Buddhist with no spouse, no bank account and no master. To him, a poem should be an anti-poem. He muses, "I have always chosen poetry whenever there was the chance for me to live a purposeful life."

Khayanpyar Htet Lu

Bago

The people aren't crude.
Nor are their principles.
Nor their history &
their resistance.

Those are hongsa sheldrakes,
leaping out of the Lapepya Lake!

Those are iron butterflies,
smashing out of hongsa bodies.

The omnipotent stupas & the palace
exude
restless souls.

 On 9 April 2021, in Bago, a city 50 miles northeast of Yangon, security forces assaulted and killed 82 people, mostly young firebrands, who put up a resistance against the junta.

Hongsa ("hintha" in Burmese) is a mythical sheldrake, a symbol of the Mon ethnic group in Myanmar. Lapepya Lake or "Leikpaya Reservoir" is a prominent feature in Bago cityscape. "Lapepya" translates to "butterfly", and it represents "soul" in the Burmese culture. "The palace" most likely refers to the seat of the ancient Mon kingdom, Hongsawadee, the present-day Bago.

Khayanpyar Htet Lu, one of the most prolific Burmese poets living in Myanmar today, manages a bookshop in Bago.

Kyi Zaw Aye

Burma's Siberia

for K Za Win

Never once
the world is on our side.

We unfurl our own flag
we unfurl our own sail
always against the wind.

The hand that signed
the statement is the hand
that will destroy the world.
I read it somewhere.

Don't look out for
a pretender to the throne.
Don't count on a saviour.
They live their life.
We have ours.

Bullets have
no address written
on them.

A knife has to
be hardened in a furnace.

The dharma begins
within oneself.

If you do your homework
there will be fewer mistakes.

Tragedy is that
the mother earth has lost a poet
who will write her history.

And still, who dare say
he wouldn't come back
like Latwe Thundra, or
Aleksandr Solzhenitsyn.

First published in *Tripwire* 18 September 2021.
Kyi Zaw Aye is a poet from Monywa. Poet K Za Win, who was killed in
a protest in Monywa on 3 March 2021, spent a night at Kyi Zaw Aye's
house on 2 March 2021. The poem is dated 14 March 2021.

Min San Wai

Hole

There's a hole the size of a pencil tip
in the bamboo wall of our house.
Not so long ago Little Daughter
piled thanaka on her cheeks and
disappeared into that hole.
She is gone for a long time.
Mother can't wait any longer.
She peeps into the hole and finds
herself looking down the barrel of a gun.
In the background is a gala dinner,
where Myanmar in blood and gore,
is chopped up and served.
At the top of the grand table sits
the phayadaka, sipping a
glass of Little Daughter's blood.
The dead wail in the darkness outside.
Mother passes out, repeating
"My little daughter, my little daughter!"
Father gets curious and looks into the hole.
Family members take turns,
peeping into that hole.
Today each and every person in this country
has a tiny hole as big as a pencil tip
in their chest.

"Thanaka", yellowish in colour, is a traditional Burmese beautifying and
skin-protection cream, made from finely ground barks of the thanaka tree.

"Phayadaka", literally pagoda donor, is someone who builds a pagoda. Pagodas are costly projects, both to build and maintain. Only Burmese monarchs and queens in the past, and Burmese generals and extremely wealthy people in present-day Myanmar, can afford a pagoda.

First published in *Adi Magazine*, Summer 2021.

The poem is dedicated to Pan Ei Phyu, a 14-year-old girl, who was killed by a bullet that came through the bamboo wall of her house in Meikhtila on 27 March 2021.

Myit Aung

Khet Thi

Each time he stepped into
our house in Shwebo
he would be dragging a big jerrycan
of peanut oil from Pale,
with the determination of a man
with a pair of single-bone forearms.
He was strong
like a waterfall.
He was a good friend
to our children.
He was a good mate
to men.
He was
a feverish lover.
He was
a star from a distant town.
O … Ko Khet Thi,
the owner of Dah peanut oil press!
How you shone, hardened and sharpened
like a dah!
Let me tell you this—
last time he came to Shwebo
he didn't bring with him
a jerrycan of peanut oil.
He pressed his own life like a peanut
and laid it down for us.

First published in Burmese at moemaka.com

ZiZiWS

A pain too close to home

YOU HAVE WALKED a long way, across historical upheaval and emotional downturn, with a soul too innocent to hate in a world incomplete without suffering. Holding onto a dream too heavy for a close-minded reality, you outlived the survival of an unjust world to share the story of a Spring Revolution.

Tell me Little Sister, what was your name?

Those beautiful eyes that danced with a longing for a safe future had missed their turn because of a sinister bullet. Blood spilled and spilled vivid beside a life let down by hate. The peaceful days you adored so much marked a memory you became a part of.

Tell me Big Sister, when they took your patient away, did you struggle, did you gasp?

For a hope that had failed, you never looked back twice. Holding on to a chance so intimate, so fragile, reciting words of Gandhi like only a believer of love and peace would, because you decided this wasn't what we deserved.

Tell me Big Brother, when injustice knocked on your door that night, did you hide in a nightmare, afraid and alone?

The CDM cost them a fortune that they used to measure our lives. The starlight stood bright between chasing reality. You were on the wrong side of another scripted lie they prided.

Tell me Little Brother, did the world you see hurt you more than the bullet in your flesh? Your call for a rescue flatlined, dead bodies piling high on an overdosed terrorscape. Uncertain, unshaken, never thought the next one could be you. Twenty-eight days couldn't wreck a soul, but it took a blinding kill and left a child orphaned. The countdown restarted, but you were never coming home, never dying again.

Tell me aunty and uncle, when your child left home that day, did you pray a little longer than usual? Waiting with your heart in your hand, lining up patiently by the door just so you could take one more glimpse. You didn't want to fall victim to a damned ego with marks of shame. So insecure you wondered why?

Behind every picture, and word, is a life we miss.

Of a human being just like us.

ZiZiWS is the nom de guerre of two Chinese-Burmese sisters who wish to remain anonymous.

#PlugX

The day your mugshot appeared on the state-owned channel

You've been gone for three months now.
Our house is quiet without you;
only the tick-tock of the old wall clock or
the playback of your favourite Paticca-samuppada sermon
by the Venerable Moegok Abbot can be heard.
Your cat stays whiney, as ever.
Since you disappeared Mother hasn't cooked
pork and roselle leaves. The bamboo mesh walls
of our house, darkened in tar, get darker.
Whenever your friends come around asking
for you, I want to smack their freaking faces.
Brother, since you were an errand boy
I knew you were a kite soaring towards the sky.
When spooled in, you felt a sleight of hand and
cut yourself loose. Then again, you always
came back. I don't like your poems. Bollocks!
After you left home, you whinged about
how you missed home in your poetry.
You wrote as if you were a worthless pebble
thrown out of the house. When Father learned
you were smoking cigarettes, he threw out
all his cigarette packs in anger and frustration.
One night, when you came home drunk,
Mother sobbed all by herself for the rest of the night.
You were like a film shown on a highway coach.

Whether I liked it or not, I was forced to watch your acts all the time.
Each time I dozed off, a noisy twist in the plot would wake me up.
In your poetry you were the *underachieving* son.
At the tip of Mother's tongue, you were a gilded paddy.
Brother, you claimed to be a communist,
but you were crazy about the Four Noble Truths.
You said you loved Soe Lwin Lwin's baritone vocal
in "Madly deeply missing you, in secret". Then again
you went to bed with a playlist of Ba Saing songs.
You were absolutely bonkers! Your whim-whams often
left your friends and us in this house dumbfounded.
Exactly three months since you've left us.
The old radio at our house looks jaded as usual.
Breakfast as usual. Mother is pushing laundry clothes
into the washing machine. Father is fiddling with the power supply.
I keep busy with damn newsfeeds and computer games.
'It has been eighteen days since he last called,"
your girlfriend complains to Mother on the phone.
There isn't a single day we don't think of you, but
the roads in our town seem to have forgotten you.
The temperature in May sears anyar region.
Under the sun all day long, leaves shrivel up.
Mother watches her favourite TV series at seven.
As if we were pulled there by some magnetic force
Father and I find ourselves in front of the telly.
At eight past eight, Mother switches to the state-owned channel.
'Bullshit, fake news!" Father and I exchange glances.
Then, our unforgettable moment!
Just as I am thinking how disgraceful the news anchor is,
your name comes out of that graceless mouth.
It's the very first time I see your photo in three months.
Brother, your face is bruised.

Brother, poet, communist, vipassana practitioner!
Found guilty of murder, terrorism and sedition
a military court has sentenced you to death.
The shock shuts our mouths, we are speechless.
Tears flow down Mother's cheeks. We are men,
but we are cowards—Father and I feel like
the sky has just collapsed. We don't know where to run.
Where are you, Brother? "A fishing village under
the scorching sun …", the opening of "Father"
by Hlwan Moe pops up in my mind to burn me more.
Each time you heard that song, you thought Father
wouldn't come home! You are older than me, and yet
you are more of a crybaby than myself. Mother's bedtime story
about a sparrow family broken apart by a storm would
make you weepy. We don't have any god to rescue you,
do we? You didn't even dare to squash a mosquito.
Now you are a murderer and a terrorist.
It's such a joke, and the joke is not funny.
Since your mugshot appeared on telly, our phones
keep ringing. Your friends want to speak out
on social media. I've lost my appetite to speak
to them. Our oddball in residence, runagate,
student who would get tipsy and serenade
at coed dorms! Aren't you also a cadre, and
a communist? You are going round in a circle
you don't even know where you really stand.
"Out of two sons, one is a revolutionary.
It's more than enough," you said.
I have no words to console our parents,
your girlfriend and your friends. No spirit medium
can guide us to you. Where are you, Brother?
The cat keeps meowing as usual.

The old radio stays old just like in our old days.
I don't know what to say when we meet again.
Mother would stay awake to open the door for you
each time you were out serenading girls late at night.
When you were out late at night I too couldn't get to sleep.
I guess I was thinking if you really were that
kindergartener who bounced, screaming
"It's a little brother, Father!", on the day I was born.
Brother, you are such a fucking dullard!

Salai Ling Pih (Mindat)

They came for Father

I hugged their knees and kowtowed to them.
They couldn't care less.
They came for Father.
The rice, scooped up, for supper
was thrown everywhere.
Mother, a soon-to-be-widow,
was beside herself.

"They came for Father.
Now we have to depend on you,"
Little Sister hugged her and cried.
We heard gunshots from the farm.

They came for Father.
Just when the farm he'd ploughed
with muscular power was about to pay off
it's all soaked in blood.

They came for Father.
Hanging at the school gate is
our national anthem,
"The equitable land of virtuous wada …"
In Father's stead,
I will have to till the land.

They came for Father.
On the earth mound of a grave

cartridge cases are still there.
Father was taxed all his life
so they could buy bullets.

Father's been taken away.
I hold Mother and Sister tight
we pray for him.

Before they come for me
I'll make sure the farm is
well furrowed—
thoroughly turned up.

"Wada" roughly translates to an ideology, an ism, or a belief system.

Suragamika

Shifting targets and the transformation of the Spring Revolution

A TARGET, as opposed to targets in archery or shooting practice, may be defined as a focal point of undesirable things. A target is not a goal. But on the way to one's goal, targets have to be overcome. The revolutionary masses must identify and overcome targets after targets to achieve their revolutionary goal.

*

The Spring Revolution was very peaceful in February. In a nationwide uprising of peoples from all walks of life, entire villages and towns took to the streets. It was very disciplined. There were donations of food, water and medicines as well as volunteer refuse collectors. "Down with the military dictatorship!" and "Recognise our votes!" were their targets. We witnessed a solidarity we never thought existed in Burmese society. Rich and poor, male and female, race and religion, those notions became redundant. Words would fail to describe the extraordinary metta or loving-kindness demonstrators showed to each other in those days. It was lively and lovely. The target of the Spring Revolution may be "Down with the military dictatorship" but the revolution does not turn its back on metta. This humane principle will remain a key characteristic of the Spring Revolution.

*

In March, the junta's response to the Spring Revolution changed. Quite often, a person who was picked up at night would have to be collected from hospital the following morning as a dead body. In the case of Zaw Myat Lynn, a community leader and teacher from Shwe Pyi Thar township in Yangon, there was more than enough evidence that unspeakable torture was involved. The authorities claimed that the detainee had fallen thirty feet to his death while trying to escape from custody. And yet his body—eyes gouged out, facial skin flayed, teeth missing, tongue blackened and melted, internal organs absent, speaks volumes about the circumstances of his horrendous death.

There was a recurrent pattern in cracking down on the protests in Yangon, Mandalay and Myaing—protesters were shot in the head or in other vital parts. The soldiers shot without warning. In cold blood, they also shot people in the back, into a crowd helter-skelter on the run. They shot at ambulances. Medical workers were beaten up while trying to collect dead bodies or help the wounded. In the case of 19-year-old Kyal Sin from Mandalay, who was shot in the head on 3 March, her body was exhumed in the middle of the night and examined to debunk the truth that she was killed by a bullet. Another pattern emerged—snipers were shooting at the barricades people had built on the streets.

That's not all. As if they were kidnappers, some security forces would demand a ransom. Many detainees were held in unspecified locations. Some detainees, usually underage students, were not properly returned to their parents upon release, but dropped off at deserted junctions in the middle of the night during the curfew. Some poor kids were usually found wandering around like zombies, too dazed to answer any queries. The junta's press briefings claimed that the kids were drug users. It is likely that a drug was force-fed or injected before their release to create an environment of fear and paranoia. In some places kids were severely beaten up during arrest and custody. This pattern is also commonplace in protest areas.

In today's digital age news travels extremely fast, and journalists became the junta's next target. There were all sorts of pressures on the free press, arrests and charges against reporters, and the media licenses of all independent local news outlets were annulled. By 17 March only two state-run papers were in print.

At the same time, the shutting down of mobile internet and Wi-Fi networks delivered a significant blow to the cyber front of the Spring Revolution. The availability of reliable news became increasingly limited for "keyboard fighters". There was an increase in the flow of the junta's propaganda, misleading information and comments. Attempts to make proposals for "social punishment" against the junta leaders and their businesses were scorned and abused by the junta's trolls. There emerged a new discourse: we should not tolerate extrajudicial killings, torture and arrests; we have the right to defend ourselves; in the face of such atrocities, an armed revolution should be a totally justifiable agenda. A call to arms became increasingly popular. The Spring Revolution was transformed.

*

The junta seems to have more targets than they can handle. Some of their responses to the crisis are not just ill-coordinated; many of them are at variance. Over one weekend, they demanded that all employees return to work on Monday. On Sunday night, however, they began to terrorise neighbourhoods with their guns, scaring anyone who might want to go back to work. They also placed blockades on the road early that Monday morning in some places, as if to stop anyone from going to work. They stop anyone in the street, seizing mobile phones in search of any suspicious online activities. They appeared to be unaware of the fact that, with the shutting down of the internet and social media being inaccessible, few people remained active online. Some of the security forces were deployed at schools and hospitals. At the same time, they demanded students and medical professionals return to schools and clinics. They accused physicians of ignoring their patients. When physicians on strike diverted their patients to private clinics and hospitals for free treatment, those clinics and hospitals were attacked or vandalised. They demanded banks to do business as usual, but they put a cap on the amount of money one can withdraw. The junta feared that public distrust in local banks, many of which were their own, would lead people to close bank accounts and withdraw all their savings. Some of the bank customers were arrested for arguing with bank employees.

They claimed they are simply trying to restore order. And yet the armed troops beat up and killed children who were at play. In Mandalay on 23 March, Khin Myo Chit, a 6-year-old girl was shot and killed as she ran into her father's arms. They seized food and beverages left behind by the demonstrators, who had to flee from their protest sites. In many towns, security forces broke into shops and houses to steal anything they could find, from drinking water bottles and tissue paper to gold and silver jewellery. They vandalised vehicles parked in the street, including ambulances. They vandalised houses too. They burned down barricades erected by the people. They set fire to some factories and houses and placed the blame on the people. The regime's targets appear to be everyone and everywhere. It didn't take long for the people to regard the junta's security forces as a terrorist organisation. They were convinced that the junta's troops were targeting ordinary citizens. The troops were killing and maiming the unarmed public as if they were engaged with enemy troops on the frontline. The junta's targets showed their own self-deception, and people learned that there was no way the alleged electoral fraud would be solved in a fair manner, no way a better democratic system they promised would come about. The military have abandoned their ethics according to which they are supposed to protect the life and livelihood of the citizens. There have been several rationales for military coups since 1962. The military's target is the people who disagree with them, and they will search and destroy anyone who disagrees with them.

*

In response to the military's position, "revolutionaries" didn't lose sight of their target, namely to impede the junta's administration with new and innovative means. With mutual understanding, support and sympathy, they were determined to sustain the momentum of the revolution as long as they could. When the shootings got out of hand, protests without people were staged. There was a protest of broken-down cars without drivers. There was a protest of pyittainghtaung, the Burmese toy similar to Tumbling Kelly. Candle light protests, protests of souls, muted protests that wouldn't provoke "a crow's caw" were also common. Night protests, protesters hoped, were staged at times when "terrorists" were not on the alert. Bazaars were on strike too.

There were talks about "self-defence", to fortify one's house and to fight back, but most people remained unarmed and engaged in peaceful protests. Nevertheless, the regime became increasingly murderous. There were an estimated fifty to seventy fatalities in a single day in Hlaingthaya township in Yangon. People were overwhelmed with grief, resentment and rage. Car tyres that were used to blockade roads were set on fire and went up in clouds of smoke, darkening the sky over Yangon. The scene in March couldn't be more different from February when streets were swept clean by volunteers after each protest. Against the backdrop of a flyover and a smoke-filled sky, people continued to give alms to the monks in the morning.

Despite the internet issue, a social media post by a physician, one of the hundreds of doctors and nurses who were engaged in the civil disobedience movement but were treating wounded protesters, was widely shared:

> "The people are amazing. There was this night curfew, but warm packages of rice and fried eggs, coconut curry noodles, and water bottles arrived overnight. They were very generous to us medical professionals. Charity ambulances and red cross volunteers wouldn't just drop off the wounded. They would also help transfer patients to relevant departments such as for X-rays. They were drenched in sweat but didn't take a break. An elderly man who was shot in the chest with blood oozing out of his wound said, 'It hurts a little.' A young man whose arm was smashed by a bullet said, 'I am okay, Sister. Please go and help more serious cases.' Another boy whose calf muscle was pierced by a bullet said, 'What a relief it isn't the shin bone.' I saw him again in the morning and offered him some money for medicine. He declined, pushing the money back into my hands. Today a man whose left arm was amputated said, 'I am feeling fine.' There are too many serious cases queuing up for the operation theatre; some people keep asking when their relatives will get treatment. But the patients themselves are amazing. No one has the heart to demand, 'Please see me first.' If these people do not overcome, who will? That's the night I saw many, many heroes in one place. (Hlaingthaya 14 March 2021)"

In all of those first-hand accounts, one could feel how people prioritise each other and help each other out in the face of threats and duress by a tremendous adversary. Between medical doctors and their helpers there were no more ranks. They all worked hand in hand. There were Buddhist nuns among the food donors. If the army was putting too much pressure on one area, people from the neighbouring quarters would come out in the street and make some noise to relieve pressure on those who were being attacked. The determination that we should suffer more so that our neighbours would suffer less was often heard in solidarity.

When the internet was blocked there were concerns over electricity outages. Electrical power staff on strike promised a continued power supply, free of charge. However, overload could lead to power cuts if too much electricity was consumed at the same time. People reminded each other, "Use electricity sparingly, only when absolutely necessary." When the Committee Representing Pyithu Hluttaw (CRPH) requested the citizens not to patronise any business that would increase military revenues people obliged. They stopped paying tax, and even stopped buying state-owned lottery. Most lottery shops went out of business overnight. When only mobile phone internet networks were blocked and cable services still provided access to the internet, those who had Wi-Fi devices at home or in their offices removed their passwords so anyone nearby could access the internet.

The masses continued to protest, without lowering their flag poles. Their target remained, "Down with the military dictatorship." Some of them began to use shields, catapults, and gas masks. There were reports of retaliation in some places. Some people were pushed to fight back by military violence. The Spring Revolution has been transformed by the atrocities that the military has inflicted on people. And yet even when treated inhumanely, we have seen that most people remained kind, generous and supportive of each other. Most people held on to their ethics and principles. On the other hand, both ethics and targets of the military council look as if a bomb has hit their heart. The masses continue to be principled, ethical and remain focused on their targets.

*

A revolution will end only when targets are hit and smashed.
The Burmese masses have proven that they are revolutionaries
capable of hitting their targets. The revolution will prevail.

Lwin (Bawtwin)

Incidents I'd rather not recall

"THERE'S A SNITCH OVER HERE! A mole!"

"Any mole in our neighbourhood? Get out! Right now!"

I have repressed these memories for a long time. I don't even want to think about them. Now I feel it's about time I say something.

In 1988, I was 18, the age of today's Generation Z. I was a student at Monywa College (Monywa University). It was the beginning of our second year. I went to College in Monywa, but I am not from Monywa. Having passed the matriculation exams in northern Shan State, next to China, I should have been at Lasho University in the region.

I was in Monywa just for the College. I wasn't that familiar with the city. I had made friends with some of my classmates, but I couldn't say they were close friends. There wasn't any friend in Monywa who knew me well since childhood. The fact that I wasn't boarding at a dormitory made my circle of friends even more limited. I was staying with my aunts. Apart from my commutes to and from the campus and my aunts' house, I had not been out and about that much in Monywa.

When the 1988 uprising came to Monywa, I couldn't just sit at home. Despite my aunts' forbidding I went to stay at the women's strike camp, headquartered at the construction sand mound at the north gate of the Phayagyi pagoda. Courageous young women from different quarters of Monywa wouldn't go home; we camped out there, staging protests, and listening to speeches. We got by with rice and curry wrapped in banana leaves sent to us by our communities. All the ladies would sleep together at the zayat shelter near the pagoda. I was at an age when one didn't think much about how worried our family members would be about our adventures. I was the only college student at the camp. Naturally, I was elected their deputy leader.

In the beginning, Monywa students didn't show up in groups. They were only organised into student protests later. I wasn't part of the Monywa University student movement. Some of my acquaintances were there, but none I knew well. Nor did I know anyone who belonged to Monywa Student Union. That's the reason I ended up at the women's camp at Phayagyi. The leader of our camp, I recall, was Ma Maw. There were male leaders in charge of our camp. They were key people who gave us guidance and protection.

I was at the camp not because I was ideologically driven or convinced of any higher cause. I was simply young and youthfully righteous. In fact, I couldn't even conceptualise the notion of democracy at that time. All I knew was that people were becoming more and more destitute under the dictatorship. We were roused to a fever pitch by what Ne Win said in a speech before he left office as the President of the Socialist Republic of the Union of Burma in 1988: "The army, being the army, does not shoot in the air." The information flow wasn't as good as today's. We relied on the short wave radio. From the *BBC* and the *VOA* we learned that hundreds of protesters were mowed down in the streets in Yangon and Sagaing.

As the movement dragged on, rumours of poisoned wells and moles milled around. Just like what's happening in the Myanmar protests in 2021.

Someone caught a "spy". The spy was tied down and met with mob justice. There was a disagreement in our leadership and splinter groups emerged. President Maung Maung, the immediate successor to Ne Win, was still in power. He would urge apologetically on radio, "Please do not get ahead of yourself." There was no way the movement would be put to an end. No one knew when and how it would end either. Protesters became worn out. Just like what's happening in 2021.

Our Phayagyi camp ended up in small groups. Some of our leaders said they were going to leave the camp, and those who would like to follow them were welcome. I went along with them. The following day I got sick and I was told to go get some rest at home. I was afraid I would be grounded if I went back to my aunties. I tried to tough it out. One of my friends at the camp suggested I rest at her sister's house if I didn't want to go home. She also informed my aunts of my situation. She saved my life.

My fever didn't come down. I felt bad that I was in the care of someone I hardly knew. I decided to go back to my aunts who gave me some sedatives, which meant that I was sleeping most of the time while trying to recuperate. Later my mother came to pick me up in Monywa. I think I must have been in bed with a fever for about two weeks.

No sooner had I returned to my mother's house in Shan State than the battle for Monywa had begun. Some of the leaders of our splinter groups were beheaded by a mob. They were "spies", "moles", "traitors" or "intelligence officers". Lord Buddha, I thought to myself, I was fortunate to have fallen sick to be safely back at home. Otherwise my own severed head would have been on a bamboo spike, a common sight in many towns in Burma during the 1988 upheavals.

No one was a mole or a traitor. We didn't even know we were labelled a treacherous group. To this day I have never done anything to betray anyone. Yet I was that close to being tried as a mole. It was utter luck that I got out alive.

These incidents I'd rather not remember. Nor do I want to talk about them with anyone. I simply cannot bring myself to think about them. I am still living with the trauma. Recently, however, I managed to talk about the events with a couple of friends, as well as about the disunity of some political movements. The breaking up of some groups can lead to

animosity, hostility and atrocious murders.
Our common enemy remains the military dictatorship.

First published in Burmese at moemaka.com, March 2021.

Ko Inwa

They don't talk big

Generation Z
arrive in the teashop.
They wear earrings.
Tattoos all over their bodies.
They are drenched in sweat.
Some of their feet
are soaked in blood.
They talk about
one of their shoes
that went off on the run.
About a
a wallet they lost.
Then they laugh.
Everything is quite light.
They talk about
how one of their phones
dropped and cracked.
How they had to flee for their life.
They laugh again.
Everything is light.
They say
"See you tomorrow."
They don't talk big.

First published in Burmese at moemaka.com, English translation first
published in *Mekong Review*, May 2021.

Moe Nwe (2001-2021)

Spring and rabid dogs

Also this spring
when cotton trees bloom again
rabid dogs are at it again.

They snarl in the street.
They attack everyone in sight.
No longer secure are
our nests.

Because you can't shoo them off
don't go beat'm up.
A pack of rabid dogs will gang up on you.

Be careful throwing a bone at
a rawboned flea-infested mongrel.
A rabid dog, a puppy or a bitch,
will bite your feeding hand.

Those animals! They are
only into sinking their teeth
into your flesh. They were born
without a conscience.

No need to go after them
because they might bite you.
Let them foam at the mouth while
cotton trees are red.

The history of this spring
has been written in blood.
Even if the rabid dogs are in retreat,
as long as the earth lives,
the curse of my tears never ends.

Moe Nwe aka Soe Naing Tun, was a 20-year-old student from Myitkyina
Technology University in Kachin State. On 25 March 2021, following a
protest in his hometown of Mohnyin, about a hundred miles southeast
of Myitkyina, Soe Naing Tun ran and hid from the security forces but
he was chased after and killed with a headshot. The poem is dated 20
February 2021.

Dr Thiha Tin Tun

My will

Just when we were expecting the best, the worst happened. State power was seized. Happy days, without fear, are over. By any means necessary, it's time to fight for the things that *cannot* be over. It's not that hard. Give us what we want, or we will fight. One by one, or two by two, we will take them down with us. My hands, that are used to holding a surgeon's scalpel, are used to blood stains.

First off, I would like to say this to Mother: In the event of my death, be proud of me. Please do not grieve far too long. Should I be killed in the struggle to restore state sovereignty, people's sovereignty, please do not grieve far too long. I would like to say this to Nan. The courage of your beloved grandson was blood-red. Just in case we meet again in the afterlife, I would like to request you to look after this grandson of yours again. Next, Father. I have never had a long conversation with Father, but I will remember Father's bond with me in what little relationship we have had. When fate dictates, our paths will cross again. Big Sister and Brother-in-law, try for a baby again. Don't give up. And Lay Thu's family. May Lay Thu live a peaceful life. And Aunty Nyein's family. You are just a family of two, but may you be in peace and harmony. Please tell U Pauk and Big Aunt to look after their health and to not let any ailment in. I don't have much to say to my friends. Of me, they will remember what there is to remember. Some of you will forget me of course. That's fine.

Love, having had a chance to know you has been one of the best experiences of my life—I can die happy with this knowledge. I believe you will understand why I am leaving you like this. Our time together was very limited. We will join in matrimony if we are destined for it. Finally, I would like to urge my comrades, who have been in the same struggle, to be resolute and relentless. Stop fighting only when people's power is restored. I am afraid I will be gone before you.

Down with the military dictatorship. Long live people's power!

Dr Thiha Tin Tun, an assistant surgeon, was 27 when he was shot in the head and killed while he was helping to set up blockades for protesters against advancing security forces in Mandalay on 27 March 2021.

Thawda Aye Lei

Whose Footfall is Loudest?

translated by Thett Su San

NEVER IN MY LIFE did I think that flip-flops could be fascinating. Only after a memorable incident entailing a particular pair of flip-flops did I begin to pay attention to them.

An incident, yes! The one that will stay with me my whole life. It made me realise that certain footwear could carry more meaning than just "footwear". It happened after Amay passed away. Before she drew her last breath, Amay had been struggling with lung cancer for nearly three months. At the time, we were living in a small town. Hoping that we could still save her, we sent her to a hospital in the city. We buried her there when she died.

Without Amay, our journey back to our small town was desolate. My heart felt empty, as if there was nothing left for me to hold on to. Everything around me went pitch dark, as if I had been pulled into a black hole. When it was decided that all of Amay's belongings would be given away to needy families, I acquiesced. I didn't want to cling to her stuff—after all, I had lost Amay as a person already. Even then, something that belonged to Amay was discovered unexpectedly. A pair of flip-flops. Under Amay's bed, lying still and quiet in the darkest corner as if they were hiding, were a pair of her flip-flops. They must have been separated from Amay when she was taken to hospital. When I looked at them carefully, I saw that the soles were worn out and the heels were ragged.

Amay was a frugal woman who always budgeted carefully and spent wisely. Apart from a new pair of flip-flops for some occasions, she wore these worn rubber flip-flops on a daily basis—when she did household chores and went grocery shopping—for many years. If the straps were broken, she would replace them with new ones herself. If only one strap of her flip-flop was broken, she would keep one new strap for later use. After several years of daily use, Amay's toeprints were impressed on the flip-flops. Tears started rolling down as I looked at them. These flip-flops showed me beyond a doubt how Amay went through hard times in her life, and how she endured pain and suffering. That pair of flip-flops I inherited from Amay would stay with me for many, many more years.

Since then, I've been drawn to stories, memories and lives that could be revealed by well-worn flip-flops. We might change clothes every day, but a member of a low-income household, who could barely afford an extra pair of flip-flops, had to rely on the only pair they had. Flip-flops were a poor person's comrades-in-arms on a thorny road. Flip-flops gave them strength. They were as close to them as their own skin.

"My flip-flops are my fortress!" poet Hla Than declared. After the military coup in February 2021, I collected more intriguing stories of flip-flops and their owners. A small, underdeveloped country suffering from economic asthma under COVID-19 was hit by a rogue political wave. This spring, the future of the nation became as blurry as the spring mist itself. If someone looked far into the future, they would only see a parched land.

The military claimed that the 2020 election fraud made the coup inevitable. Prior to the election, "The Sound of Heels", an election campaign song by the National League for Democracy (NLD), was very popular. It became the NLD's triumphant anthem following the party's landslide victory in the election, but it vanished into thin air after the military seized power. The song was dedicated to the State Counsellor, Daw Aung San Suu Kyi, leader of the NLD, to whom her supporters referred as "Amay". The song was about how her efforts gave Myanmar, an ostracised society under long years of military rule, a chance to step onto the world stage. On 1 February, the clack-clack of heels were silenced by the bang-bang of military boots.

Before long, the whole country was completely under the boots. The voices of mourning mothers, the tongue-clicking of dismayed youth, the moaning of farmers out of their stubbled fields and workers out of their factories got louder and louder each day. "Join the CDM now!" As soon as the rally cry put people on alert, all those different voices merged together—ineffectual whines turned into battle cries reverberating across the sky.

If someone had ever questioned whether footwear could be frightening, the answer would have been "yes", if they were military boots. In the first week of the Spring Revolution, civil servants joined the CDM en masse. The main action of the CDM was that no employee should go to work. In some political cartoons, military generals in jackboots trampled doctors, school teachers and workers. "Stop going to office, struggle out of the dictatorship!" was the slogan of the strikers. They warned each other that if people continued to work for the military state, many precious lives, beautiful things and human values would be smashed under the boots.

That's how footwear became a central character in the Myanmar Spring Revolution. There was more to come. Within a week of the coup, thousands of young people took to the streets. In response, the military hired a group of jingoists and staged counter-protests. Some anti-coup protesters started shouting that they were out on the street on their own volition, and that they had not been paid by anyone. To drive home the point that they were from well-to-do families and that they could not possibly be bought, they came to the protests in expensive outfits and shoes. This, however, only highlighted the dire situation of most of their fellow protestors, who couldn't afford fancy outfits.

There were messages on social media condemning some affluent protesters for talking down to people from underprivileged backgrounds, including those hired by the military. In opposing tyranny, people simultaneously learned to smash any form of discrimination based on wealth or class.

Day by day, the revolution gathered strength. It soon turned into a nationwide protest of people from all walks of life—rural and urban. Their footfall echoed in the streets. Now street surfaces seemed totally covered by an array of flip-flops and shoes that it would be difficult for anyone to gain a foothold there. Spring was in full bloom. On roads where fallen ones would be laid to rest, columns after columns of rallies continued to march over and over again.

One of the non-violent protests was known as "Lace your shoes up!" In the early days of the Spring, security personnel seemed uncertain about whether they should use force against protesters. They tried to push the crowds off the roads, saying the people were obstructing traffic. The youth reacted by making their protests mobile. They moved around in small groups and continued to protest.

They crossed the road when the light was green. They stopped when the light turned red. They shouted rally cries. As soon as they had the chance, they sat on the road, lacing up their shoes at a leisurely pace. Policemen watching them were speechless. In the following days, there were "harvesting onion" and "collecting rice grains" movements. Loose onions and grains of rice were deliberately poured out in the middle of a road so everyone could help pick them up and put them back in the bags to annoy the police. Spring flowers of a variety of colours were seen everywhere. New and creative forms of revolutionary activities shone here and there.

Some people found fault with these kinds of protests. Young people were not serious, they said. Others pointed out the generation gap. Older people did not understand the state-of-the-art techniques of young people. In reality in the early days of the spring, people of all ages managed to build mutual trust and solidarity. They were full of energy, enjoying the calm before a storm.

The fresh, green spring would soon turn into a fully-blown parched summer. The intense heat made wall tiles rise up and crack. A heatwave also pervaded throughout the democracy movement. The forces standing up hand-in-hand against the junta were hit with a bloody gust. A volley of gunfire across the sky set a flock of roosting birds on a chaotic flight. A group of soldiers and police chased down the protesters who were retreating into a neighbourhood, and like blood-starved beasts beat them to death. Even the black asphalt road began to weep, blood streaming down all over her face.

After blood was spilled, the style of people's revolutionary art also changed. Each time a group of people were chased by guns and batons, dozens of ownerless flip-flops would be left abandoned on the street. Some flip-flops were upside down, others in the gutter, and many of them unpaired. And yet most of them looked well-worn. When the security forces were gone, people picked them up and organised them in pairs for their owners to come and collect them. The abandoned flip-flops didn't look great but they could be invaluable to their owners.

In this way I learned, rather accidentally, that flip-flops had always been important witnesses to our revolutions. In the 1988 uprising, flip-flops were scattered everywhere on the road. In the 2007 Saffron Revolution, there were many flip-flops drenched in blood. Following the 2015 student protests, hundreds of flip-flops were on the road again.

There was even a shoe charity campaign in 2021. It emerged after some people began to question on social media what kind of shoes would be most suitable for protests if they were to escape from violent attacks. A number of shoe donors came forward. In some places, many pairs of "used, feel free to take" shoes in various sizes were on offer. Some people who owned extra pairs of shoes shared them with their comrades. They exchanged metta in sharing shoes. They looked after each other. They became more united, realising that people were cut from the same cloth.

On top of physical violence, people also suffered from psychological warfare by the regime. The longer a revolution dragged on, the more volatile revolutionary morale could become. And yet, crackdowns notwithstanding, most protesters decided to continue with their struggle. Some bid final farewell to their parents and friends. "In the event that I am killed I donate my organs to anyone in need," some people wrote in their wills.

"Don't push this person any further, / at land's end / my flip-flops are my fortress," read the last lines of a poem by Hla Than. People prepared for a last-ditch fight. Oaths—that they would not back down no matter what—were sworn. They glued pictures of the coup leader on the roads and marched on them. The senior general's face was smeared with hundreds of footprints.

The murder of protesters became more commonplace. The number of martyrs multiplied every day. People shed new tears before old tears dried on their cheeks. They were placed under curfew. Internet access was restricted. Arrests and detentions under various charges became more frequent. People felt less and less secure. There were no more grounds for them to take a stand, so it seemed. They became afraid of nightfall. What they feared more probably was the nightfall over their future.

One day I saw a photo of a pair of slippers on social media. "These belonged to a mother. They were left during a protest." They were white and size 37. The straps were white, but not pure white. The left and right slipper must have been thrown into disarray when the wearer was attacked. There was a line of blood on the pavement that stained one of them. I learned that the owner was a 50-year-old school teacher. She was shot to death at that spot by the military terrorists. A bullet that hit her hand took her life as she had a heart condition.

"She wasn't feeling very well when she went to the protest," said her daughter in an interview. The alleged "2020 election fraud" brought dishonour to members of the education department who had overseen the polling stations. That's why she believed that it was her duty to protest the coup on the front line. Before she left home, she had comforted her daughter that the security forces would go easy and not use violence against school teachers.

Sadly, the gun barrel does not discriminate—it was loyal only to the finger that pulled the trigger. One bullet after another shattered our dreams. Karl Marx's slogan "Proletarians have nothing to lose but their chains," echoed loudly among the masses.

The daughter wept violently over the slippers left by her fallen mother. This reminded me of how I cried whenever I saw my amay's flip-flops. What of her? Would she become interested in footwear too? In revolutions, footwear is often prematurely parted from its wearers.

The group in military boots stood firm, determined to put an end to the civilian resistance. The people had no weapons, nor sturdy shields. Their flip-flops wore thin. Even then, the hot, bloody roads couldn't be worse than hell. No one seemed to mind the intense heat under their soles.

With or without footwear, their way out of hell would be an arduous journey.

Hla Than's poem, translated by Ko Ko Thett.
The Burmese writer Thawda Aye Lei has published four novels and two short story collections. She is currently working as a researcher on gender- and media-related studies for Burma-based international NGOs. In 2021, she enrolled in the PhD program in Political Science at McMaster University, Canada.

Mya Zinyaw

The Bank

My second cousin, Father's niece, phoned me from our village the other day. She was unwell. Her husband, an immigrant worker in a neighbouring country, wanted to wire some money into my bank account. She requested me to withdraw the money for her and retrieve their gold jewellery at the pawnshop in town.

I wished I didn't have to go to any bank during these days. The military regime had put a cap on the amount of cash one could take out at any local bank lest the country's economy collapse if people withdrew all their savings at the same time. But she was Father's niece! She looked after our house at the village as we lived in the town nearby.

Once our whole family came down with a fever. She came to stay with us and obliged to arrange for much of Father's craving for mouth-watering dishes—from carp with mushroom and bamboo shoots to pounded Indian gooseberry with sweet soup and haritaki fruits to go with grilled ngapi. She had always come to our rescue many times in the past. Now that she was unwell, I didn't have the heart to turn her down.

I went to the bank and enquired if I could withdraw cash on my cousin's behalf, and, if so, how much I could take out in a week. The teller said, "You can withdraw the money. It depends on our manager whether you can withdraw 5 lakh kyat or 8 lakh kyat at a time." I wasn't very pleased, to say the least. My cousin's husband would transfer 15 lakh kyat (about 830 USD in September 2021). It would take three visits to the bank if I could withdraw 5 lakh at a time. To avoid having to visit the bank many times, I asked my cousin's husband to wire the money to three different individuals— Father, Mother and myself. After we received a notice from the bank that the money had arrived for us, Father, Mother and I marched up to the bank as if we were in for an important military operation.

We knew that we had to submit our national identity cards to form a queue at the bank. We were at the bank at 9:15 am. There were already fifty customers ahead of us! The bank was on a busy thoroughfare opposite the town market. There was a traffic jam in front of the bank, due to a profusion of pedestrians and passing cars, amidst motorcycles parked on both sides of the road. In the meantime, there were more and more people appearing at the bank. Observing social distancing of 6 feet was simply impossible in a crowd where one could touch the next person at the stretch of one's fingers. There were around a hundred people waiting outside the bank, sitting on their own motorcycles, standing between motorcycles, or taking shade from the scorching sun under the Indian almond trees that lined the road.

We scanned our surroundings for a place less packed. There wasn't anyone near the bank security shed, so we went there to take a look. We weren't surprised to find that the spot was a rain-filled pothole covered with broken Indian almond twigs for a "caution" sign. Into it betel quid was spat, plastic was trashed. Not at all a very hygienic place. We returned to be with the crowd. If we had been too concerned about our own safety, then we would have simply returned home.

Everyone was wearing a face covering. "What is there to be afraid of," I steeled myself. Moments later I heard someone next to me "ptui!" and spat on the ground. I saw a man pull down his face covering, expose his mouth and spit betel quid onto the street. After that he pulled up his face covering, adjusted it with his hands and continued to chew the quid. After a while he repeated the same "ptui!" and the same sequence of acts. I decided to turn my back to him. Now I was facing two women who seemed to be lost in their own world of chit-chat. They would pull their face coverings down to speak. When one was speaking with her face covering down, the other would listen with her face covering on. All the while they took turns speaking and listening, their mouths and hands kept busy.

Then a young Buddhist monk appeared and handed out empty envelopes that read, "I have come here in person to raise funds for a new learning hall at Hnit Oo monastery." Under that line was a list of prices—for a bag of cement, a box of sand, a truck of bricks, and a sheet of corrugated iron. Under the list was "May you be well. May you be charitable. Thadu, Thadu, Thadu." Some people declined the envelope quietly. They simply shook their heads. Some people received the envelope but did not place any contribution in it. Only two persons next to me put some money into their envelopes. The first one, 200 kyat (around 10 cents USD). The second one, 500 kyat (around 27 cents USD).

A moment later I saw a lady walk past us towards the bank teller to present her identity card. There were several women like her, but that particular lady appeared very meek. She lowered her head and bent her back and knees in a gesture of respect in front of the teller. Only after the teller accepted her identity card and gave her a nod of approval did she right herself. "Aw …" I felt speechless, and somehow saddened. When I looked at the place where the lady was sitting, I heard another lady on the phone, "Yes. Only one of us received the transfer. Not both of us. The money was wired to both of us at the same time. This happened before. We dread the disease but we now have to come to town every single day. Tell your husband not to send more money for the time being. Uh…okay okay, if that's the case he might as well send more money right now."

Just when I was thinking, "Not easy at all!" a bank teller came out carrying a pack of identity cards in his hand, calling out names. He called ten customers at a time. The customers whose names were called could enter the bank and withdraw cash. All of those who heard their names called smiled as the people around them looked on with envy. I had no idea how long they had been waiting at the bank. Very diligent people. One had to be diligent during these difficult times. There were people whose names were called but who were not able to withdraw money. The money for them wasn't ready, or had not arrived yet. They were told to come back the following day. How disappointed they must have been after such anticipation!

Those whose names had not been called yet were not allowed into the bank premises, let alone the bank building itself. Two young guards would open the gate to let ten people in at a time and shut it with a bang once the people were in. For good measure they locked the gate, too. "Oh boys, we wouldn't enter the bank if you said NO!" I was proven wrong. Soon an old lady pushed herself through the crowd and through the gate. She succeeded. Soon she emerged again, grimaced. She was told that she had to submit her identity card like all other customers. Awww… some people!

It was almost noon and the sun was trying to melt us right down from the top of our heads. No more shade under the Indian almond trees. Some people began to sit down. Some people squatted reluctantly while others simply sat their whole bodies down on their flip-flops. As for myself, I thought I had to wait in the sun for the shade. I was still wearing a motorcycle helmet. Beads of sweat formed all over my face, but I didn't dare to wipe them off with my hands. My hands had been all over the place in the past few hours. It would be detrimental to touch my face with my hands. My ears became itchy at the same time—what a dukkha! I looked around to see everyone around me soaked in sweat.

Earlier this morning when people saw a bank teller coming out with a pack of identity cards in his hand, people would get excited. They would think their names would be called out. They would gather around the teller to pay attention. Only when they learned that their names were not on the list did they return to where they were. I'd been here for two hours and people didn't look very excited, even when they saw the teller come out of the bank. Sometimes a person's name was called and he or she wasn't paying attention, and people around them would have to yell their name out. People who got bored began to drink water or juice, munch on snacks, gaze at an empty space, or busy themselves with their phones. I, too, got very thirsty under the sun and all I could think of was going home.

I had been waiting since 9:15 am. My name wasn't called until 11:30 am. On my feet for hours, and sweating profusely, I began to feel a heat headache. I thought my name would be called by 11:45 am. Then a bank teller called my name. I felt so grateful, I thought the bank teller was my saviour. "Take the helmet off, and wash your hands," he commanded. Once inside the bank I enjoyed the air-conditioning. There were ten plastic chairs for customers, each about four feet apart. It dawned on me that people were packed outside the bank so only ten customers could enter and observe social distancing inside the bank.

There were plastic protection screens in front of the bank employees. The actual cash withdrawal took no more than five minutes. For that moment we waited nearly three hours. I was very thrilled when the cash was handed to us. Even a lottery winner wouldn't have been as joyous as me.

In this country it made us happy when we received our own money as a reward for our long and laborious waits.

First published in Burmese at moemaka.com

Zeyar Lynn

Portrait of 'The Need for Oxygen'

I don't want to walk around downtown any more.
An unspeakable-invisible evil is making the rounds.
Perhaps it's crawling up the Traders-Shangri La hotel?
The Pansodan overpass reeks of its fishy stench.
I focus around Sule Pagoda. There're no more
waves of people, only the roar of a gust trampling
on the void of a desert, a stupa with a broken spire,
a mosque stooping its minaret, a church with both
eyes shut for good. The city centre used to be
around here, wasn't it? I can't believe it,
this place was teeming with life before! I look up
towards the City Hall. A pitch-black shadow dodges
my gaze and disappears into the building. There's
no more President Hill at the President Hill.
The river breeze is muted and choked with sadness.
The disoriented burial ground doesn't know where to go.
Frozen with the footfall of the Japanese Occupation
it just squats down in the middle of the road.
The pigeons on the wire get scared and fly away,
towards the past. A colonial horse, ready to stomp
on Bo Aung Kyaw Road, raises its forelegs.
Is the fire still ablaze in the city's chest? As if to prolong
grief, the clonk-clonk-clonks of executioner jackboots
are back on the staircases of the Secretariat.
Where a road rests at a strand, the Strand brims with
chronicles. I lend an ear to the thud-thud-thuds from
somewhere. Is that invisible heart still beating?

Is the big wound still hidden? The downcast
Independence Obelisk looks inside its empty self.
No matter what,
tomorrow will come to town. Where shall we meet?
Don't you think I am exaggerating, my friends!
Café de la Rotonde is expecting us, just as
Saya Mya and Ilya Ehrenburg in the Fall of Paris.

15 May post-coup 2021.

Bo Aung Kyaw Road in downtown Rangoon/Yangon is named after student activist Bo Aung Kyaw who was killed and, consequently martyred, in a protest by a mounted charge from the British Indian Imperial Police in 1938. In response to Bo Aung Kyaw's death, Ba Hein, a Marxist student leader then in Thawaddi prison, declared "A horse foot stomping will set the Revolution ablaze."

Saya Mya refers to the much-loved Burmese author and translator Mya Than Tint (1929–1998) who published a Burmese translation of *The Fall of Paris* by Ilya Ehrenburg.

Zeyar Lynn

Portrait of 'Coming Soon'

In broad daylight,
running through a field ablaze,
a man on fire!

In a pedicure-manicure salon,
in a shaded study, reading news, or
in anxiety, thinking of my next meal,

I try not to look, but
I know he's charging right at me.

The water
in my cupped hands
trembles.

28 May post-coup 2021.

Zeyar Lynn

Portrait of 'Door to Door'

They smashed the whole shrine.

They didn't find the homemade
explosives they were after—
just a termite trail on the wall.

"Back off, you all!
We've had a tip-off."

On the floor is the protection Buddha,
His glass body in two pieces,
His glass head in smithereens.

Bootprints,
all over the walls and the floor
of the prayer room.

And now—who will intone
the Metta Sutta tonight?

25 April post-coup 2021.
It is customary for Burmese Buddhists to recite Metta Sutta as a way of
spreading metta, or "loving-kindness", to all living beings in the cosmos.
The three portrait poems by Zeyar Lynn were first published in the
inaugural issue of *PR&TA*, October 2021.

Ba Maung

Staying tuned

I look out
from the edge of the woods.

I see
black clouds of smoke rising from my village
rolling through the sky—

towards the past.

First published in Burmese at moemaka.com
The poem is dated 26 June 2021.

Thida Shania

An ox for a wad of paan

What does this air suffer from?
My lungs suffocate when I breathe.

Why does the sun look desolate?
There is twilight without dawn.

How can I satiate hunger?
An ox swapped for a wad of paan.

Where can I hide my body?
Corpses, everywhere in every house.

How can I die in my land?
My kin have been buried alive.

How can I cross the border?
Rivers bleed human blood.

What happened to the Queen of Justice?
I search for her everywhere—
nowhere do I find her.

Thida Shania is a Rohingya youth poet, artist and mother. Her poems have been featured in *I Am a Rohingya* (edited by James Byrne and Shehzar Doja) and other anthologies. She usually publishes her poems and drawings at the Art Garden Rohingya website.

Tun Lin Soe

In the Yoma foothills

It was one of those foggy mornings.
As if they were offering a wreath
to a squad of soldiers off to war,
a flock of birds sent me off with chirrups.
That's how I began my flight—
full of doubt.

My beloved parents,
brothers and sisters,
relatives from near and far,
childhood friends who stay friends to this day,
and above all, my girlfriend, my heart of hearts,
for each of the teardrops they shed
I was responsible.

Now that I'd left them
my soul got restless,
my spirit drained of vigour
I wept for hours.
The tall trees in the jungle
witnessed my creaky-creaky cries.

I thanked them all,
those who pushed me onto a raft upstream to drown,
those who abased themselves before me,
and those who, possessed with greed,
lifted me higher so they could shove me off a cliff,

and those who loved me back,
I thanked them all.

I thanked God
for keeping me safe in the wilderness.
He heard my prayers
those nights and days
in the Yoma foothills.

Tun Lin Soe, a Rohingya poet, was born in 1987, in Min Gyi Ywa (Tula Toli) in Maung Daw, Rakhine State, Myanmar. He was a final year English major at Sittway University, when a pogrom against the Rakhine muslim population broke out in Sittwe in June 2012. At the end of 2012, his name was on a list of arrest warrants for 30 people, accused of colluding with insurgent groups and international media outlets. Since 2013 he has been living in Malaysia as a refugee.

Jo Zaw

Long distance runners

Since the gun blasted
we keep running & running,
front, middle & back.

We traverse boobytraps of punji stakes,
rivers, streams, cliffs, gorges,

lions, serpents, tigers, insects,
crocodiles & hyenas
in the shower of hunters' bullets.

We run and run, but
where?

Jo Zaw is a physician and a writer, known for his short stories since the
1980s. The poem alludes to the 2020 Tokyo Olympic Games. The poem
is dated 2 August 2021.

Lynn Nway Eain

Mausoleums

When this spring is over
there must be a mausoleum
in every village and every town.

This is no neighbourhood fire.
This is civil war.

This is not about
a flat and a car for a family.
This is about 60 million people,
their right to live like humans.

This is not about a new division.
This is about a whole new state.

Even when you peel onions or pound chillies
tears may trickle down your cheeks.
Revolution is not a walk in the park.

Every country of dignity
has to fight for their own freedom.

In our new state
in every village and every town,
there must be schools,
hospitals,
religious buildings for all sorts of worshippers

theatres, concert halls and opera houses
for working people,
parks for children and
gardens for lovers.

Above all,
when this spring is over
in every village and every town
there must be a mausoleum.

First published in *Tripwire*, 18 September 2021.
Lynn Nway Eain is a Burmese poet, based in Maryland, USA. The
poem was first published in Burmese at moemaka.com on 8 April 2021.

လီလီပန်းကို ခွေးဟောင်တယ်

လီလီပန်းဟာ   အံချဉ်ရုရု
လီလီပန်းဟာ   ကိုးကဆီပျိုယ်နဲ့.သူ
လီလီပန်းဟာ   သံခင်းတာမန်ခင်း မှုသာ မဟုတ်ဘူး။ "

လီလီပန်းကို ခွေးဟောင်တယ်
လီလီ ပန်းကလေ
သူက လီလီပန်းလေးဆိုတော့.
ခွေးဟောင်တာလည်း ဆန်းတာဘူး။ "

ခွေးကတော့ ဟောင်ပြဲ ဟောင်တယ်
နွဲ့ဆိုတော့, ခွေးကလှုပ်လှုပ်တယ်
လှုပ်လှုပ်တယ်
လီလီယှဉ်ကလေးကတော့.
ဆကားတခုနဲ့ ပြောဘာတယ်
ဘာသာတခုနဲ့ ဘာကလှုပ်ဖျွ လှုပ်ရွဆွာတဲ။ ~

ခက်သီ

2020–2010

A grassy earth mound of a grave,
tomorrow
is buried right there.

Thitsar Ni (b.1946)

Ohnmar Myint

Poet K Za Win

My brother's birth name was Maung Chantha. He was born on 24 May 1982 to U Kyaw Sway and Daw Win May in Letpadaung Village, Salin Township, Sagaing Division. He was the eldest of four siblings, the pride of the family.

In 1992, he finished as one of the top ten students in the region in the fourth grade national exam. Despite parents and teachers wishing that he continue at a high school, he decided to study the sasana, the teaching of the Buddha as a monk.

As he wasn't old enough even to be a novice, he became a boarding student at the village monastery. Later he studied with religious rigour at renowned monasteries for Buddhist studies in Monywa, Mandalay and Bago.

He was a distinguished young Buddhist scholar, earning the title of Ganawasaka Sasana Alinkara Kyaw at the Thamanay Kyaw centre for Buddhist teaching in Bago. As a monk he passed the BA level studies in Buddhism, but declined to take the exams for the title of Dharma Sariya, a title similar to an MA. He said he didn't want to be honoured by the military government. He started to oppose the military rule as a monk around that time.

After three years as a monk, in order to pursue a literary career, he left the sangha, the order of the monks. Since he was a little boy he was overly fond of reading. He grew up reading beyond his age. He wrote verses. Unlike most other kids who spent most of their childhood playing, he was reading most of the time. He was a taciturn kid. When he talked he was brief and straightforward. Since he was young, he would stand up for the underdog and for what he believed was the truth.

My brother, as a child, was also very good at making clay figurines out of red mud from the Chindwin bank at the village. The clay toys he made were so intricate even adults admired them. He would make different animals and things he saw around him: elephants, horses, oxen, people, cars, carts. Once he even fashioned a diesel water pump out of clay, a luxury item in our village.

Years later we would tease him that because he spent most of his childhood reading and making mud toys, and because he wasn't a physically active kid, he wasn't developed physically as much as he should have been, and was shorter than anyone his age. He took this to heart and would tell any parents he knew not to mind their children running about. He also encouraged children to read. He devoted much energy into building the very first library in our home village.

Mainly for participating in a student protest in 2015, he was indicted on five charges, found guilty and sentenced to one year and two months at Thaywaddy Prison.

And now, in 2021 in Monywa, while he was at the forefront of a nation-wide protest against the military coup, representing the Myanmar Poets Union, Union of Myanmar Youth Poets and All-Burma Students Front, he was shot in the head. I believe he was still alive when he was dragged into an interrogation centre. He must have been tortured to death.

Ohnmar Myint is a school teacher and K Za Win's sister.

K Za Win (1982–2021)

The clarion call of a rainbow

Right now,
to my country and parents,
and to that young lady
I am in love with,
I am a rainbow
ensnared on the horizon.

In this country
during the dark days that
gang-rape us,
like a warrior off to war
brandishing a dah
I am out in the street
with my dah poem.

I am fearless.
I am fussy.
I am firm.
I am unsteady.

Like a crocodile
I've crawled,
my chest firm on the earth.
Like an ape
I've hopped from one branch to another,
only to grab the air.

In this country
where the majority is filthy-poor
and a minority is filthy-rich
it gives me no pleasure
to be a patriot.
No pleasure
to love my parents.
No pleasure
to fall for that young lady.

None of my prayers,
nor playing with myself,
gives me no pleasure.

Like a weed that grows
in the tundra
I've come of age.
I look back at myself
my country and
my friends
for over thirty years.

From the Buddha
and pongyis
to panhandlers
I look back at all of them.

Everywhere I look
I see fish in the fish traps.

I can't help, but see
the welt of dukkha,

the Noble Truth,
festering with pus and blood.

I can't see
our own faces.

The rainbow that's gone haywire
has given up their identity.
So have I.

I've learned
to oppose pagoda donors,
whose names are inscribed in stone.
It is the masses
who lay bricks for their pagodas.

I've learned to
hurl fuck yous at
the army and the affluent
who ride both left and right shoulders of
my land
when I am tipsy.

What else can I do?

On such a spacious land
our humanness is limited.
Our rights are limited.
Our freedom is limited.

Our landscapes
do not go beyond the hills,

stationed with snipers.
Limits are everywhere.

And still
our people through the ages
have bored through unjust limits.
They have bored through the pages.
They have bored through the classrooms.
They have bored through the factories.
They have bored through the paddies.
They have bored through the roads!

Parents
who've bored through
won't be home for their children.

Children
who have bored through
won't be home for their parents.

Students
who have bored through
won't come back to classrooms.

Labourers
who have bored through
won't return to their carving knives and chisels.

Peasants
who have bored through
won't return to their ploughs.

People on the street
who have bored through
have bored through the depths of an abyss and
will never return.

Blood
breaks out at every corner.

In the Age of Bankruptcy
no wonder
our beliefs have gone bankrupt.

No wonder the arahatta daza,
the banner of the sangha,
the saffron robe of the monks,
stamped flat under the army boots
on an asphalt road prays,
"Long live the President."

The demon Mara,
who has stolen the Buddha for fifty years,
waves the sword of evil in fits of delirium
until his very last breath.

The machine of the ignoble
foams at the mouth.

O the Most Noble King,
He who is blessed to become the future Buddha,
He who has kicked in the face of the Metta Sutta,
don't you dare touch my country
with your dirty hands!

I, the poet in chains, command you!

"Fear makes
injustice feel at home."
Rise, mates, rise,
let's bore through the blood thirst
of despotism.
Let's bore through it again.

Let's embark on a long march.
Let's march again.

Let's yank the failed state
out of the not-so-funny gags of the politicians.
The tongues of their gaungbaungs
flap shamelessly in the air!
Let's yank it out again!

Just like the loggers who
will cut the branches of a tree
before felling it, let's put on trial first
the two nefarious classes
behind the Mara mechanism.

To see a rabbit out of a hat
we put up with the mumbo jumbo
of the magician for over fifty years.
In the end we let that rabbit
guard our carrot farm.
Years and years were wasted.

Down with congenital authoritarianism.

The despot is decomposing alive.
The fish-saucy smell of his rotten corpse
stinks to high heaven all over the country.

Spring fruits
in the orchard of the insane
are infected with worms and maggots
before the harvest.

Our war is no longer
a war against a foe that we can eliminate like a foe.
Our foe is pretending to be our friend;
the hands that have killed the sangha
are building many a stupa.

As the Buddha prophesied,
"udakamanyay ardatetan …",
water is on fire.

O the venerable, the Vexillum of the Nation,
you might be able to forgive the jackboots
who have trampled on your shaven heads.
No matter what, could you please
not leave the Buddha's words,
"ma pamar datta bikeway…",
under those boots.

C'mon, mates!
Let's exorcise
the evil spirit that has
possessed our land.

There is a long dark night
between the dawn of democracy
and the dusk of despotism, a time when you can't tell
your blood brothers from strangers.
Let's ring our bell to that truth.

C'mon, mates!
Let's wake from the nightmare,
the nightmare gifted to us by
those who possess us.

Let's set fire
to the fake spring
that refuses to obey orders
from the people.

Take out the tainted flesh
from the feast of the people
and bury it for good.

Set the revolution alight,
let us be as brave as Prometheus,
let's sacrifice ourselves!

C'mon, mates!
Resist the devilish
temptations.

Like Spartiates
at the Battle of Thermopylae
let's get rid of defeatism,
let's make a last stand.

The way we hold on to our swords,
let's hold on to our blood-red creed.

To my country and
my parents,
to the young lady I love,
and to my friends,
I send my untethered love
wrapped in a poem
like a clarion call from a god.

O people
the day has arrived!
It's time you
enhance your sumptuous feast
with justice flavour!

First published in *Index on Censorship*, Summer 2021. Excerpts of the poem published in *Mekong Review*, May 2021.

K Za Win (1982–2021)

A letter from a jail cell

Dear Father,
the River, whose stomach
was cut open,
has declared war
on our tiny house on the bank, hasn't she?
Right in front of the house
you must be looking out for someone
who will help you with
embankment poles
to straighten the river,
to fill her holes with
sandbags.
In the murky water,
which rises like a bamboo lance,
you must be gazing at
the sesame plantation—
laden with fruits
ready for harvest.
You must be thinking
a fistful of rice in your mouth
is about to be fingered out.
Maybe you will find solace
in religion, contemplating
our five foes.
Maybe you will
think of the void
a son's labour can fill.
One son, two daughters and one son;
The eldest is a poet in prison,

the first daughter, a school teacher,
the second, a graduate in the kitchen,
the youngest, a student.
Your poet son,
is he even employable
as the dah you use to clear weed?
Forgive nothing, Father.
Nothing!
"Son, Pho Chan,
why do I hear noises behind you?"
you asked on the phone.
"I am at the bus stop
to post a manuscript to a journal," I lied.
From your liar son in the dock
to thugs who sweeten you
with the tips of their tongues,
"To our benefactor peasants …,"
because they want to have you from behind,
hate them all, Father.
Hate them all.
A thief is
unarmed.
A thug is
armed to the teeth.
If thieves are ungovernable,
if thugs are ungovernable,
what's the point of government?
Whatever happens to the jungles
whatever happens to the mountains
whatever happens to the rivers
they don't care.
They love the country
just the way they love to grate a coconut,
from inside out,
for coconut milk.

Plinth by plinth, to make their throne taller,
they will point their guns at the urna
on the Lord Buddha's forehead.
Their class is that crass.
To cuss at that class
if your religion forbids you
allow me to lose that religion.
I will turn the air blue
on your behalf.
Maybe you don't know yet.
Your son was
set up
for demanding the so-called police
not to harm ordinary citizens.
Someday
your son, who is not a thief
nor a thug
will become employable,
good as your dah that clears weed.
For now, Father,
keep gazing at the plantation
you'd ploughed with your naked shoulders.
Keep singing
the anthem of
The Peasant Union.

Yours ever,
K Za Win
Cell 1, Section 10
Thayawaddy Prison

Published in *Mekong Review,* May 2021; *Journal of Peasant Studies,* May
2021; and *Tripwire,* 18 September 2021.

San Nyein Oo

Khet Thi: Iron fist in a velvet glove

I.

THE IMAGE OF an iron fist in a velvet glove popped up in my mind as soon as I heard my friend Khet Thi had fallen at the hands of the junta inquisitors. Poet Dagon Taya used the phrase to describe his friend, the anti-colonial student leader Ba Hein (1917-1946). We both loved Dagon Taya. If he knew I was placing him on the same pedestal with the legendary Ba Hein, he might decline the honour in his usual self-conscious manner.

Khet Thi as a person may not have been as velvety as Ba Hein. Khet Thi as a poet was. Ba Hein was a carbine-toting communist guerrilla for Burma's independence. Khet Thi became a guerrilla leader armed with what he had, an outdated tumi musket, in the 2021 revolt against the Myanmar junta.

"A youth without leftism is useless," wrote Hanthawaddy U Win Tin. Khet Thi was a youth with a lot of leftism. So was the poet K Za Win, who was martyred in the early days of spring. Khet Thi, a native of Pale township in Sagaing region, was not into the Communist Party of Burma (CPB). He was in sympathy with the Red Flag Communist Party (RFCP), a radical group that emerged out of the 1946 CPB split. Khet Thi told me once that he'd prefer to be a red flag, like his grandfather. K Za Win and Khet Thi's departure left me with a pang of pain in my heart—they were beloved poets of the 'northwest plains of Burma', my heroes who had swam upstream against the roaring Chindwin.

II.

Khet Thi passed away on 9 May 2021, just a day before Dagon Taya's birthday, which is a literary event in Myanmar. "They shoot in the head. They have no idea the revolution dwells in the heart." Khet Thi wrote those lines in the days when many protesters were dying from headshots by the junta marksmen.

On 8 May 2021, at around 9 pm, he was snatched by a group of armed men who worked for the terrorist junta. He was dead within twenty four hours after his arrest. His body was released from Monywa mortuary the following day. I heard that his wife, who was arrested together with him and held for a few hours, had to try very hard to get his body back.

In the first week of that May I talked to him on the phone to discuss if we should commemorate Dagon Taya's birthday in our own ways under the circumstances. I raised the idea that we could start a political campaign on Taya's birthday. "I am not really keen. Not that I don't respect him, but what I am doing now is an armed struggle. Dagon Taya was a man for non-violence. I feel bad," he said. "Taya was not totally against armed struggle. He would not engage in a violent conflict, but he wouldn't oppose those who did for the right reason. That's how I understood him," I reasoned with him.

A few days after that conversation he was dead, and I found myself fleeing for my life, like a leaf swept away by the wind. My longing for him was most acute on 10 May.

> "In the revolution
> Don't let them know what you do.
> Don't let them know your whereabouts.
> Only when you've fallen
> after a successful campaign,
> let them learn your name."

Those lines by Ho Chi Minh in *Ba Hein Blood*, a pamphlet published by my comrades at an insurgent outpost where I live now, remind me of Khet Thi again. Very few people knew what he did and where he was in the Spring Revolution. He was seen giving speeches at some anti-coup protests in February, but he disappeared after K Za Win's funeral in early March. I learned from my phone that he was toughening himself up to wage a guerrilla war against the regime troops in his region. Only some of his comrades and friends may have known what he was really doing.

It's not easy to write about Khet Thi. The Revolution is not over yet. I am aware that I should be discreet. Still I would like to write how great a man Khet Thi was from my perspective, and how I miss him sorely. In these unpredictable times nothing is certain. I myself am facing uncertain tomorrows. To write about him is to allow my pen to possess me.

After I heard of his passing, I lamented out loud, "Khet Thi, my friend, did you come here to *string hard* truths with your own life for the liberation of our people?" His name "Thi" translates to "to string" and Khet means "hard" or "difficult". I solemnly saluted the great foot soldier of the Spring Revolution, the commander of a clandestine armed uprising, who had sacrificed his own life to protect his people. I wept.

III.

"When you are enslaved under a wielding sword, if you don't have the courage to draw your own sword in defence, history will judge that you deserve to be a slave," said Bamaw Tin Aung, a senior monk, who was an erstwhile prisoner of conscience, and I tried to talk Khet Thi out of the armed struggle. We thought it was too early to take up arms. He didn't agree. Even when there were peaceful protests nationwide, he told me on the phone, "I've made up my mind. I am convinced that they are not going to be swayed by protests alone." At that time, I didn't know why but a military group was after me. I started moving from one hideout to another. "Just be careful. In the end, it's likely that our only option will be armed struggle. I don't object to a friend's idea," I told him.

I came to understand that Khet Thi was keeping very busy. He was ahead of others in thinking of a guerrilla war against the junta. That's probably why they've killed him with such enmity.

Lest we forget, armed revolutions have always played a critical role in our anti-colonial and anti-fascist struggles, and the country's independence.

IV.

You can't shoo a tiger off with a wisp. You have to shoot it. Khet Thi was no tiger tamer.

> "On this hillside tigers abound,
> stick around, my love, on my hunt
> for bamboo shoots."

"Taking the Vow", the couplet by Kyi Aung, was one of Khet Thi's favourites. "My wife puts up with me a great deal. She only forbids my drinking. In fact, she is my comrade." The poem reminds me of Ma Chaw Su, Khet Thi's wife.

Khet Thi was a tall and stout person, a giant with a huge square face. "I say I am a poet. But my art is quite insufficient. I am always seeing red," was his self-critique. "Oh really? I was a fan of your poems even before you were published in magazines. Your composition is special, your thoughts and diction are unique," I told him. "Makes me happy when you say that." His square face beamed like a kid.

Maw Min Thann, the Mandalay poet and classical guitarist who died from COVID-19 in late July 2021, fondly referred to

Khet Thi as "the poet with 10 Ps face", alluding to the squarish shape of the obsolete Burmese 10 Pyars coins from the socialist era. How I miss Maw Min Thann and his wit too. Khet Thi had a wilful and cranky side, but he was simply being himself.

After graduating from the Government Technical Institute (GTI), he worked as an engineer for a while at the municipal department for border areas. He was one year my junior at the GTI. We both loved the literary power couple, Ne Win Myint and Khin Khin Htoo, and we had a discussion about their work in the months before Khet Thi died.

Those who didn't know Khet Thi thought the poet was full of himself, but once they got to know him, they would learn that his imagination and thoughts didn't really match his manners and come to love him. When Khet Thi passed away I talked to the Monywa poet Kyi Zaw Aye on the phone. We both felt a huge blow after we lost both K Za Win and Khet Thi.

Kyi Zaw Aye and Khet Thi didn't get along. They appeared to be rivals in the close-knit Monywa poetry scene, but the feud between them was more like that between schoolchildren at a playground. "I love to make arch remarks about Kyi. I like pulling his leg simply because he doesn't like his leg being pulled," Khet Thi said. I love both of them and I had tried to broker peace for them. Now Kyi Zaw Aye was sad beyond words.

V.

Khet Thi in my mind's eye brings back the memory of a number of other poets and friends: Thit Nyein and Thit Kaung Eain, poet Hla Than and his wife Ma Chaw, Aung Ba Nyo and Lu Eain, Ko Noe, Hein Myat Zaw and Khin Zaw Myint. Monywa poets Ko Than Tun, Maung Pei, Tun Ko, Nyi Nyi Hlaing Oo, Min Nyein Chan, Lynn Moe Swe and Naung Naung. Also Ma Lwin.

This year our generation, which came of age in the 1990s, has been on the high seas, grappling with rains, tempests and tsunamis. One after another, some of us have left. Heading for another life seems as easy as a walk back home.

What a horrible year for poetry! So many of us have fallen, our days filled with dukkha. Unflinching characters as they are, poets from all over the country fought against the junta on the frontline. K Za Win, Thet Nyein Thit, Maung Khin Hmaing (Chauk), Loi Lwan, and Khet Thi are gone. The imprisoned are Yawnathan, Maung Yu Py, Moe Oo Swe Nyein, Pai Thitnwe, Han Lynn, Than Tint, etc. The former two remain in jail. The latter were released in July 2021.

Some of us have become outlaws, living a gruelling life. Our poems are to be found in the "Liberated Area" where the struggle to free the country from military slavery continues. Our poems!

VI.

Survival

I don't want to be a hero,
I don't want to be a martyr,
I don't want to be a coward.

I don't want to be a reckless fool,
I don't want to be a milk-and-water person,
I don't want to humiliate myself.

I've seen freedom of speech whose tongue was cut out.
I've lived with human rights behind bars.
I've survived many a sterilised day.
Let's end our own hell—with our own efforts.

I don't want to be the cream of a politician.
I don't want to be an armchair poet.
I don't want to support the Adharma.

If there's just one minute left for me
I want my soul to live that minute clean.

Khet Thi
14 February 2021

VII.

One evening Khet Thi and I were together. He had a few drinks. I didn't drink. Before bedtime we were lying in the same bed, and we both went online. "Shall we write a poem together? I haven't collaborated with anyone. I am in the mood now." A message popped up from "Khet Thu", Khet Thi's social media account.

"What?" I thought to myself. I was lying right next to him and he had sent me a message from his phone. I gave him a look but didn't say anything. As I kept quiet, he didn't push me further. He went quiet too.

I had no idea it would be our last meeting. Had I known that I would have been much obliged. I began to write;
In my half of the poem I miss you.
For you I will write now, my friend
[…]

Khet Thi (1976–2021)

What a bummer!

Here's the update;
The government that deserves a lot of F-words is voted out,
the government we should not fuck with is voted in.
People who've lived in the same shithole for so long
long for a change of course.
Even the spirit mediums, when they want to please their wild spir
sing, "Mother Suu must win."
Any news?
Blackouts and
Consumer goods prices
continue to repress the luckless.
Any news?
News is
We are not chicken any more.
Today's propaganda is a bit more pleasing to our ears.
The new government looks honest—or so we think.
Yesterday we were spooked by the Stasi.
Today it's the Lobbyists we must fear.
Yesterday we were spooked by the Thugs.
Today it's the Idiots we must fear.
One thing in common the Thugs and the Idiots have;
"Dare you touch our government.
I'll club you to death!"
Yesterday they did club you to death.
Today they club you to death on-air.
What a bummer!
I believe

The government that deserves a lot of F-words
Reduced us to rags.
The government we should not fuck with
Will make us rich, hopefully.
So I believe.
So they too believe.
What a bummer!
When the Idiots gloat over nothing,
The dignity of the government we should not fuck with is downsized.
A real bummer!
I am not happy.

First published in Burmese at moemaka.com 28 April 2016.

Poet Khet Thi, from Pale township, Sagaing region, and his wife Chaw Su were arrested by security forces in the afternoon on 8 May 2021 in Shwebo, Sagaing, where they lived. Chaw Su was released within hours of arrest but Khet Thi's body, internal organs missing, was returned to Monywa mortuary in Sagaing the following day.

Khet Thi (1976-2021)

The grand gorges of Yangon

There are black holes in space.
Into the bargain
We have Grand Gorges in Yangon.
The Bargaya Gorge has sunk Yangon
Along with her history.
We & hip-hop kids are still buried in the Bargaya Gorge.
When propane springs forth from the Rakhine littoral towards Ch
We mine the Gorge for cooking gas.
There wasn't enough gas that would have killed Sylvia Plath.
Incredibly deep are the Grand Gorges of Yangon.
Incredibly thick is the darkness trapped inside the Grand Gorges.
Bread is in the Grand Gorge of Evil.
It is baked in the Inferno.
Once, a girl who wanted to go abroad to become a housemaid
Was sucked up into the Grand Gorge of Evil.
There are several Grand Gorges like that in Yangon.
The Grand Gorges whistle; they wait for you.
The Grand Gorges wear Darling's Grace headdress; they wait for y
A Grand Gorge, in flare jeans, leans against a power pole.
Hanging a cigarette at the corner of his mouth in the style of
A classic gangster, he waits for you.
A Grand Gorge will gorge another Grand Gorge that will gorge y
    another one.
They smile & wait to see if one will buy another's snare.
The Grand Gorges of Yangon are
Made in China. They don't last long.
They tend to disappear, only

To pop up in another place.
The number of people who have fallen into the Grand Gorges
    of Yangon
Are ten times that of Beijing's population.
Yangon has turned into a restless &
Sleepless conurbation.
Sports cars no longer race in Yangon nights.
Yangonites must now pay attention to the noises coming out of
    the Grand Gorges.
What do they hear?
They hear snakes hiss.
They hear bones crow.
They hear a singalong out of the Grand Gorges.
The residents of the Grand Gorges are singing together.
Their anthem gets livelier and livelier.
Peoples of the Grand Gorges step on each other's
Shoulders to climb up to the surface.
With their voices in unison
They boom "L'Internationale,"
Raising their fists towards heavens.

First published in *Tripwire* 18 September 2021.

Khet Thi (1976–2021)

A letter from a caveman

for Ko Than Tun

Exhausted with a front crawl across hell
I hitched a speedboat ride.
I had no idea
my shortcutism would sink me even faster.
I gave a pat on my lap
I shot up in the air
I kneed the firmament.
I thought I was fab.
I had no idea
when hubris slapped me in the nape
I would have to hang my head.
Even when falling topsy-turvy
from a high wire
I blew a flying kiss to my fans—
I was a circus act.
I had no idea
real friends have to be panned like gold
in dukkha.
Now I know
antidepressants
don't really cure the downhearted.
You can't put out a fire in your chest
by fleeing into an accelerant.
In the last-ditch fight with my own shadow
if I can't kill it, I know, it will kill me.

I dig through the depths of an abyss
to look into my own chest.
I find my body and soul ablaze.
If not for metta,
I would have been reduced to ashes.
Where are you?
Where are you?
I look for myself.
Forced to prescribe a meaning to my own existence,
Ethic equals Empathy is what I've learned.
Just for a moment,
The tightrope tends to snap quite often.
Just for a moment,
I am still changing the burden cable.
I will be back.
Heroically, I will be back.
Not a hero who will knee the heavens in the groin,
the hero who will kneel down
to kiss the earth.
When we meet again
won't you repress "Nice seeing you again"
with your usual sardonic smile;
"About you we haven't any tattle."

First published in *Index on Censorship*, Summer 2021.
The poem is dedicated to the influential Monywa poet Ko Than Tun, a former political prisoner and Myanmar national literature award laureate.

Ko Ko Thett

My Sad Captains: K Za Win and Khet Thi

ON 4 MARCH 2021 I received an email from a poet friend in Monywa, Myanmar: "Just bringing you some sad news. Yesterday, K Za Win was killed at the anti-coup protest near Phayani in Monywa."

I was totally shell-shocked. It was only in January that I translated K Za Win's poem, "A Letter from a Jail Cell". I was pleased when the poet emailed to tell me he loved my translation. When I translated "Talking with the Taxman about Poetry" by Vladimir Mayakovsky into Burmese, K Za Win's poetry was pretty much on my mind. Now the poet is dead.

Since the military coup in the beginning of February to the end of April more than 700 protesters were killed in protests all over Myanmar. A number of the victims were tortured to death in custody all over Myanmar. In the face of violence, peaceful protests transformed into "self-defence" by the people. K Za Win, and another Monywa poet Kyi Lin Aye, were some of the earliest fatalities on 3 March, when people had not resorted to fighting back with whatever homemade arms and ammunition they had.

All of his young adult life K Za Win was a Buddhist monk. He left the sangha, the order of the Buddhist monks, arguing that being recognised as a learned monk by the Myanmar military state would be pointless. He became a land rights activist, as his family, along with hundreds of other peasant families in Latpadaung near Monywa, fell victim to land grabbing by China-owned Wanbao Mining in collusion with Myanmar authorities.

When he joined a university student rally in 2015, he was not a student, but he marched with the students along the 350 miles-route from Mandalay to Yangon for education reforms until the rally was cracked down near Yangon and most student leaders, and himself, were arrested and jailed. He spent one year and a month in prison, after which he published his best-known work, a collection of long-form poems, *My Reply to Ramon.*

K Za Win was a volunteer Burmese language teacher besides being a poet. In the 2020 election, he said, he didn't even vote for the National League for Democracy (NLD), whose policies he was very critical of, but when the NLD won a landslide and an election fraud was alleged as an excuse for the 2021 military coup, he found himself at the frontline of the anti-coup protests. K Za Win was just one among many people who have laid down their lives for what they thought was a fight worth giving their lives to. Many hundreds more, including poets and writers, have also ended up in jail just for dissenting against the coup.

Myanmar has never been a properly functional state, especially in the rural ethnic regions where civil war has hardly ceased since the country's independence in 1948. In 2021, however, the civil-military conflict has spread to towns and urban centres in mainland Myanmar. In the words of the poet, who does not want to be named, who informed me about K Za Win's passing wrote to me on 5 May:

"In Myanmar the situation is that both the junta and the people are moving towards the front line for war. 'Will war happen today or tomorrow?', everyone anticipates. Innate kindness of people has disappeared. In its place is a sense of rage and retaliation. The people who used to express sympathy even for an injured animal they found on the street like to ogle gruesome pictures of dead policemen and soldiers on social media these days. They look happy watching those pictures. I don't think

I am qualified to decide whether or not one should look forward to a war. But everyone seems like they would want a war as the only way out of an increasingly tightened space—with the belief that for a ray of light a gun can blast off a pitch-black sky."

The pitch-black sky couldn't get darker when I heard the news that another poet friend of mine, Khet Thi, was snatched by the security forces in Shwebo on 8 March. Khet's Thi's body—internal organs missing, was returned to Monywa mortuary within twelve hours of his arrest on 9 March. Like K Za Win, Khet Thi was a key figure in the Monywa poetry scene. I got to know him in Monywa when I returned to Myanmar in 2014 for a poetry anthology.

He had this poetic and physical presence, that at first seemed standoffish, but when you got to know him you knew he was gentle and kind to the point of vulnerability. A "hard-shelled nut", he called himself. In 2015 me and my girlfriend ended up visiting his house in Pale overnight for poetry, guitar singalong and bootleg whiskey. Khet Thi's parents operate a rudimentary peanut oil press for local peasants, something I had never seen before.

American poet Christopher Merrill read one of Khet Thi's poems and commented that Khet Thi was "Frank O'Hara met Osip Mandelstam in Mandalay." As far as I know he was the only Bama poet who has written a poem, dedicated to the 2017 Gu Tar Pyin massacre of Rohingya people by the Burmese army.

Both K Za Win and Khet Thi were very generous with me reading their lines. Translating them, I can exercise my poetic imagination. When I lived in Sagaing in 2017, Khet Thi would give me wake-up calls at 4 am sometimes, tipsy and lonely perhaps. I regret I switched the phone off to be able to sleep after a couple of wee hours calls from him. He got married after we came to the UK in 2018.

Perhaps the following lines by Khet Thi speak for my sad captains:

I will be back.
Heroically, I will be back.
Not a hero who will knee the firmament in the groin.
The hero who will kneel down
to kiss the earth.

First published in *Tripwire*, September 2021.

D Lugalay

Death is not the end

A bird just died midflight—
its journey half-done
& now in midair
it has just taken
the last breath.
The remaining journey
for the lifeless bird is
the distance between
earth and heaven.
The bird is done with dying,
but not flying.
On earth, however,
death usually means the end.
Then again,
there's exception

First published in *Cyphers Magazine* 2017.

Paing Soe Wai (1944-2020)

Football team

I will have to go to the local
to remember my own name.
All of us are left-footed, and level-headed—
we are reincarnations
of violent spirits, the result of violent deaths.
Let's hit the bottle
so we can talk about those
who've died from drinking.
Next
we will knock back our own past.
Train of regrets will pass.
Like cicadas, who drone on
until their chests burst open,
we, the open-chested, will booze
until our chests break apart at the seam.
We haven't scored a single goal in
"How to make friends and influence people."
Let's launch a flurry of imagined free kicks into that book.
I have yet to bump into Napoleon, the man.
Cheers, cheers!
We haven't defeated Manchester United.
Cheers, cheers!
We won't call on any port!
We won't pull up anywhere!
Cheers!
It's closing time.
It's time for own goal?

Keep your puke in your own pocket.
Flip-flops are getting mismatched.
Am I wearing one of yours?
You mine?
It's time to shoulder our own ears, and
go our own ways.
Will you open the door, love?
Is there any voice in the music today?

First published in Burmese in *Tharaphu Magazine*, November 2001.

Moe Kyaw Thu

Pai Thitnwe

He always carries a knapsack
full of hooks.
He will hook you up with the Renaissance poet Natshinnaung.
He will hook you up with the post-modern poet Bogyi.
For poetry his car is always at the ready.
He will come walking to you
with his feet in the air.

His hard drive brims with worms,
texts that can barely be read, and
flowers that bloomed and wilted yesterday.
There's no place for him in his own bed.
It's lined with books
written by you and me.

He is a light glacier,
a heavy warmth.
He will always refuel our fire engines.

In the dread of night
he can walk from Sanchaung to Thakayta.
There is no night-sitter's bed at the hospital
which doesn't recognise his name.
His honesty is super authentic
it's punchable.
He is an evening always
drowning in sweat.

When you happen to meet him,
you will notice a green water bottle tied
to the side of his knapsack.
He piggybacks that bottle
just to quench your thirst.

Pait Thitnwe is one of the poets snatched by security forces at a protest in Yangon on 27 March 2021. Released from Insein jail, 1 July 2021. The poem is dated 16 April 2019.

Moe Kyaw Thu is the chairperson of the Myanmar Poets' Union in 2021.

Ko Ko Thett

Remembering Lynn Moe Swe (1976–2017)

The funeral I wrote down happens today.
Or, does it?
The opening lines of "Until the end of the wake" by Lynn Moe Swe anticipate afterlife. Lynn Moe Swe, who died of Dylan-Thomas Syndrome aka alcohol poisoning in the wee hours of Monday, 18 September 2017 in his hometown Monywa, was one of Myanmar's most outstanding poets of his generation. He was 41.

> The hard-to-attain human life is
> as fragile as an earthen pot. They're about to smash
> that same old Buddhist cliché all over again.

How long does it take to booze oneself to death in contemporary Myanmar? The answer is five months, according to Lynn. Since April, Lynn had been drinking a type of moonshine widely known as BE, which has seedy origins in the socialist-era Burma Economic Development Corporation (BEDC). Monywa poets are known for both Thomasesque boozing and rowdy language. Lynn, however, was extremely introverted and introspective, very much like his finely crafted poems.

Lynn was a high school teacher when he wasn't writing poems. The pattern of his drinking showed that he would drink excessively for two to three months, usually during the school holidays from around February to April. He would hardly write poems during the boozy season. In recent months though, he started drinking in April and the brake on alcoholism had failed to the extent that he was often seen drinking at his favourite

BE shop during school hours.

Poet Tun Ko, his pal, said that Lynn had four girlfriends or so—one of whom, an engineer from Dubai, happened to be in Myanmar and attended his funeral—a neat smart phone for social media, a fine motorcycle for his commutes, and had no obvious reason for self-destruction. Above all else, Lynn was obviously in love with the inferior BE and would wash his face in it first thing in the morning. Each time after he collected his high school teacher salary, he would pay a month advance to the BE shop so he could patronise it without money worry until his next salary.

His mother told me that he would usually listen if she told him to quit, but he would walk out on her in his final weeks. In a desperate attempt to discipline Lynn, the mother even considered asking Lynn's boss, the headmistress of his school, to lay him off. Lynn was very fond of baseball caps. He was always seen wearing a cap, and had a collection of about 15 caps. He lost all of them—one at a time, during his intoxicated sprees, added his father. A day before, a private hospital in Monywa had declared Lynn, who had been in coma for five days, brain-dead. When he was carried home by his parents and poet friends, his heart was still pounding.

They linger over the goner.

They eulogise him as if he were a twitching leaf floating in the wind.

"Is he really dead? He looks as if he were asleep?"

The fact that the poet's heart outlived his brain for a few hours gave family and friends a shimmer of hope that he might wake up again.

Their wails fester.

What if he could hear "Well done, well done, well done!"
at the end of the sermon?

What if he wakes up and walks again?

What if he wakes up and quips,

"Didn't I look dead when I was asleep?"

While Lynn's body lay in wake at his home for around 12 hours, a typical Burmese concrete tomb was hastily built for him at a cemetery nearby. By 5 pm on the same day of his death, the funeral procession, a few cars and dozens of scooters, three wreaths from three different Myanmar poets organisations and one from a Monywa library where he was a volunteer, headed for the cemetery. Upon arrival at the cemetery, each member of the funeral procession received a small plastic bag containing a drinking water bottle, and packets of washing detergent and shampoo from Lynn's family members and friends. Lest one should be soiled with death, it is customary to wash oneself after a burial service in Myanmar. In the cemetery pavilion, a team of monks gave a send-off sermon to Lynn and those who survived. After the sermon, the monks left and Lynn was carried off towards his freshly-built tomb.

In the entombment, the coffin, carried by a number of his friends and relatives, was simply placed in the huge tomb, much like a matchstick drawer pushed into a matchbox, and sealed off with brick and mortar. At his funeral no earthen pot was smashed. One of his colleagues from his school read out an order terminating him from his duties. Another from a public library where he was a volunteer relieved him of his responsibilities.

The last time I heard from Lynn Moe Swe was on 14 April 2017 when he emailed me the manuscript of his new collection of 50 poems. Perhaps he wanted me to translate the poems, but was too shy to ask? The brief entombment concluded when a friend of Lynn took a twig, and announced that his soul would be welcome back to the family home for a stay before it decided to wander off again as exactly Lynn Moe Swe has written down:

Once a burial is done,
no one turns back at the graveyard.

Both the living and the dead must
hurry home.
How come the black hounds don't howl today?
A tiny twig has just replaced a man.

First published in *BLARB*, the *Los Angeles Review of Books*, 10
September 2017.

Lynn Moe Swe (1976–2017)

10:10 o'clock

Wellbeing has nothing to do with an
on-off switch.
Blackout persists in other towns. As for me
the weatherman who usually starts with,
"Howdy, my dear friends?" has been with me all day today.
Shot with an arrow of time
here's a young man in any-way-the-wind-blows outfit,
an adolescent flag flapping in a gale.
In such a starlit darkness
you no longer have to croon, "Oh, my darling, oh, my full moon!"
The climax where the police are
arrested by the police has yet to arrive.
It took only thirty comrades to establish
the Myanmar Armed Forces.
They are doing just fine without you.
I am too busy to look up at the donor climbing up the pole of
his own charity marquee.
Protests are making rounds like novitiates on horseback.
Since anything can turn into a mass movement any moment,
my backpack is
my office now.
No wonder the country is at the roadside—
on the road
you often bump into that bloke
who says, "You guys are roadies' roadies."
If you can tell
a throw-away

from a slip-away
this poem
can go on, or
end right here.

First published in *Cimarron Review*, November 2017.

Lynn Moe Swe (1976–2017)

Stream gauge for peace

It's the talk of the many—
very few have been there.

Opium blooms under the title;
My own stomach asks for it.

Craving for a stupa each time you see a hilltop?
It must be a side effect of Buddhist chauvinism.

Parochialism lives here.
So does cordite smell, in cherry blossoms.
Like a waterfall that cannot curb its own speed,
we've flown into ourselves.

If you know nothing of a river's highs and lows,
you should not blame the rapid Salween.

In private
she keeps quiet.
In public
she keeps quiet too.
She doesn't know
the Bamar word for virgin.
When asked,
"Was it a Bamar soldier?"
She simply sobbed, and
nodded.

They've come to school,
wearing no shoes,
having no legs.
The landmines are
nowhere to be found.

Peace rests on a *peace* of paper.
You know no peace.
We know no peace.

First published in *Mekong Review*, November 2017.

Lynn Mar O (1983–2018)

Mi Phyu [Missy White]

That distant echo of a yelp
I just heard,
was it you, Missy White?
Since that day
I didn't get to nose your punani
I've been yowling ceaselessly.
The stones they've thrown at me add
an overtime of pain
to my heart in melancholy hell.
The beef bone securely hidden for you
in the jungle flame hedge
in front of your house—
is a symbol of my love.
With an elephantine intrigue
I snatched it at the wet market.
The butcher's viss weight got me in the ribs.
On the ground under the hummingbird tree
you'll find my claw marks.
They are your portrait.
If you don't believe me
go sniff at the rear left tyre of
your master's car.
My piss will
smell of my longings.

Maung Saungkha

Who is that guy?

I've just shaken his hand, but
I don't know who he is.
Looking left and looking right
I cross the road with a very busy mind
investigating my own past,
where that guy might have played a part.
Who is that guy? Who is that guy?
I am on my way to my girlfriend.
All I am thinking all the way
to my girlfriend is that guy.
When I mistook him for someone else
that guy said, "You are mistaken."
Since I am such a smooth person
I just smiled, pretending nothing happened.
The guy didn't introduce himself.
He left me questioning myself,
"Who is that guy? Who is that guy?"
Come on! Come on!
I get really tired, running in circles
after my own thoughts.
Now I need a drink.
My freaking money is spent on water, but
I still don't know who that guy is.
Come on!
Walk on, and think hard.
Look left and right and try to recall who he is.
I am dying to see my girlfriend, but

I must remember who he is.
I've even unlocked my phone unnecessarily,
thinking who that guy really might be.
Because of that guy, I find myself
unintentionally gawking at the backside of a woman
who is walking in front of me.
When I meet my girlfriend
the first thing I tell her is about that guy.
I can't keep him out of my mind.
The guy follows us into the bus.
At the love hotel, thinking of that guy,
I walk straight into my favourite room without checking in.
I was almost humiliated.
"What's up with you today? You are not yourself."
At the end of my girlfriend's remark,
the guy pops up in front of me again.
I cannot *not* think of that guy.
I try to lock him out,
but he has already locked me in.
Caressing my girlfriend's breasts
I am thinking of that guy.
After we have sex I lie down flat on my back to relax.
Guess what!
That fucking arsehole is standing right over me!

First published in *Modern Poetry in Translation*, Focus on LGBTQ+
poetry, 2018.

Maung Saungkha

Image

On my manhood rests
a tattoo portrait of
Mr President.

My beloved wife
found that out after we wed.
She was utterly disgusted,
inconsolable.

In 2015, Maung Saung Kha was jailed six months for penning "Image".
In 2021, after the coup, after taking part in several protests, Maung
Saung Kha fled from his native Yangon to take up arms against the junta.

Maw Min Thann (1971-2021)

September

City gates are shut.
The thoroughfares
are quiet.

The pandemic threatens
individual lives.
War is not over yet.

September—
friends,
mates,
lovers,
I long for them from a distance.
I converse with them from a distance.
From a distance
I remember them.

September—
in an arid afternoon
I find myself alone,
like a ghost.

In a flash
I miss you.
I send metta to you;
may you be well,

from a distance.

Maw Min Thann (1971–2021), classical guitarist, writer and poet, passed away from COVID-19 in his hometown of Mandalay on 29 July 2021. His guitar performances often accompanied poetry readings in Mandalay. The poem, dated 13 September 2020, was written during the first wave of COVID-19 and the lockdown in Mandalay.

Han Lynn

When I perfume myself

When I perfume myself, my twenty feet ambit exudes musk.
Wrapped in the fragrance, I walk about in crowded places.
My attar surely turns heads in front of me. It also turns heads
behind me. Myself? I just keep strolling, walking on in sweet-
ness, pleased, but embarrassed.

First published in *Poetry International*, February 2015.

Han Lynn

Elevator

The coffin doesn't fit
in the elevator.
Let's keep it vertical.

The body will
be standing.

Isn't a coffin always
too heavy? Shall we put
this one on wheels?

A coffin pusher
wanted

in an elevator
going down
in a high-rise.

Han Lynn was one of the poets snatched by security forces at a protest
in Yangon on 27 March 2021. Released from Insein jail, 1 July 2021.
First published in *Poetry International*, February 2015.

Maung Phone Myint

Asses for the Masses

According to surveys
The masses who have accidentally smashed into fala
Have abandoned their cyclone aid clothes
That do not fit their constitution
The voice of the masses must be heard in the
Implementation of federalism for
The asses of the masses
In the upper regions of Chindwin & Monywa
The cattle of the masses are already pissing
Through a hole in the back of their house
Into the urinal tracks of SEA Games
The opposition who have agreed in principle
To toe the toad in principle says
They will support the bill in earnest
Nationalism is the sixth column
In the genuine XXX union
That will consolidate the asses of the masses
The foundation has not been laid yet
Partly because
The asses of the masses are not firm yet
When a party colludes with another
& blows a rubber
Peter, in the face of the masses,
Becomes a parliamentary erect for the masses
A nail is driven into the thigh of the masses
Another, into their ass.

The Commission for the History of the Asses of the Masses
Has been approved
For the monkeys in must
In the midst of a storm
The masses who do not know how to react
When the Allies in all grandeur enter them
Simply croon their national anthem
"The Grandeur" in unison
No Committee is available to answer
the paramount question from the masses:
How can we fuck your ass back?
The masses are a damaged condom
Between the cliff of cronyism
& the opposition in the establishment
It has become an additional duty
Of the masses who grind their teeth & moan
"Tough it out. We are simply in the wrong age."
To tough out the tyranny of the civil society
In all holes of their communities
It's also an absolute norm for the masses
To step back another line, so
Their country won't step back
As the good masses, we only know
How to wag our head in approval
As such, in each & each age,
The masses & the asses, the asses & the masses
Are synonymous
I heard it has always been that way
Since the twilight years
Of the Konbaung Dynasty.

"Fala" is Yangon slang that was popular in the 2010s. It means "enjoying
a free ride or a freebie."

Thar Lu

Girl

This morning, Little Brother said he was off
to school. He came back this afternoon
in pieces. Not even his school bag was with him.
He was carried home by a Samaritan.
How broken-down Little Brother was!
His head and entrails in one plastic bag. The rest in another.
Those black bin bags! Exactly the same type we
use in our town. We checked his body parts. One of his
legs and his two fingers weren't there. There was
a ring mark on his left middle finger. The ring was missing.
I was very upset.
No, not about Little Brother's death. I was upset with
Mother's incessant weeping. I was pissed off by her eye water.
She wept the same way when Dad died. I was very annoyed
that time too. This sort of thing happens in our region every day.
There's no point in declaring today special. I told that
to Mother. She said, "You will go to hell."
So what? Here and now, worse than hell.
Take this—for years, I've been with
a man who often sucks me for blood.
If you ask me about my bruises, you will have to
smell my sweat. Or maybe I will let you have a taste
of my blood? There's no water and blood inside me.
My body is filled with semen.
Sometimes Mother came up with,
"My husband no longer loves me. You are his love now."
That's true.

Her husband can hardly wait for my menses to stop.
I have two kids now. The second one is still in my tummy.
Mother also said,
"You are a slut. That's why you have to go through all this."
What can I say? Each time I go to bed, I ask myself,
"Is this place hell or human?"
Whenever Mother's husband crawls into my bed, it's hell for sure.
Mother simply lets it all happen with her arms folded.
Now Mother is weeping for her son's death.
I will watch her, with my arms folded.
Little Brother had stepped on a landmine. Why wasn't the foot that
stepped on the mine my own?
I always think about that when I walk.
If there's a mine in my way, I would go step on it.
Now I have to go to school. To learn A, B, C.
When you learn to write your own name
you can at least sign your kids off at an orphanage.
No way I will leave my kids with Mother.
The person I trust the least in this whole world is
Mother.

First published in *Hnin Si Phyu*, Vol. 1, No. 4.

Maw Shein Win

Factory

blindfold wound around a bleeding head
sepia timecards & combination locks

sound of coworkers arguing in the bathroom
or the other way around

crows captured in dim light
murder mystery for a limited audience

pupils of soft brazen green
lacquerware box in an abandoned mall

factory workers assembling cell phones & wheelchairs
a scorpion in the break room

Maw Shein Win

Restaurant

I recognise her voice because it's my voice
I don't know that name because it's his name
I think your voice has a name but it's my name
she met herself in a restaurant

it wasn't her restaurant but it was a place she had been before
she had eaten eggs there, Potatoes Anna
the dishes had no names
the waiter had a high voice

how could you not remember me? we were married last May
the cakes were baked by professionals
one of them looked like a marvelous dress
what will you bring to the table? what is your sir, name? what are
the camels doing here?
please, change, for, me

are those your wind chimes?

From *Storage Space for the Spirit House* by Maw Shein Win, Omnidawn, California, 2020. The poems also appeared in *Mekong Review*, February 2021.
Maw Shein Win is a Burmese-American poet based in the Bay Area, San Francisco. She is the first poet laureate of El Cerrito, California (2016–2018). She often collaborates with visual artists, musicians and other writers.

Mae Yway

In the ballpark

you get girly-jealous/ you are a blabbermouth/ your shyness
shuts your cute eyelashes/ to become a couple, you have
the right to say "yes"/ you are an erratic driver/ everyone
is born free and equal except when you are born short of
decent karma/ you say your son is your Lord, your God,
your husband/ you have womanly tricks up your sleeve/ you
cheat/ you slut/ all your life you are kept unmolested under
the heavy thanaka grinding stone/ you deserve a bride price/
you are wed-&-fed to him/ you walk three steps down your
house & you don't manage to get back home/ you are a
single-mother-to-be/ your given name follows your family
name/ you are just a slave on his path to the Buddhahood/
your whole life is cooking in the kitchen/ you are busy
fancying a reliable man/ a man shouldn't grimace like a
woman/ a wife has to dog her husband/ you are always at the
lower end of the seesaw so the other end could stay high/ you
are thin with intellect/ you act second sex/ to protect your
pussy is always your first priority/ don't rape me, please/ I am
just an entertainment/ just a dependent/ I have no right to
lead this household/ this poem writes this poet/.

Mae Yway

Pretence

No one wants to be weepy.
Each time I hear a name,
I wonder which list it's from—
from the register of the dead,
or the survived.
Tiny little insects, which live for a day
to go away in the night, may be mocking us,
our ephemeral lives!
The deceased or the living?
Where shall I write their name down?
Whose name will be published
on what side of my memory?
How long will it last?
Will it be washed away with soap?
Will it be clawed out with scabs?
If I can't have chicken, can I have pork?
In this country, that's become a celebrity
of a country all the world over,
a chicken egg may be a cele while it lasts.
Things must be preserved in resin.
When corpses were piling up,
fortunately, shall we just say "fortunately",
while the crematorium was available for a while
my uncle turned into smoke.
I was happy-sad.
'happy' or 'sad',
I didn't know where to begin.
I hid behind a face covering
I got away for a while.

Mae Yway's first book of poetry *Courier* appeared in 2013; the second *You & I* appeared in 2016. In 2017, she founded the poetry publishing house 90/91, while working as a digital content strategist and TV writer. As of autumn 2021, she has left Myanmar for a residency at the International Writing Program at the University of Iowa, USA.

Maung Yu Py

A poem for real

Only those
backed up by strongboxes
make love after love after love.
As for me,
I am with a token of a girlfriend.

Having to endure life is real.
I don't know why
I am Charlie Chaplinette over and over again.

Lest someone should thieve,
the plastic cup is chained
to the charity drinking water tap,
exactly the kind of installation art
the age demands.

This year too
Asia's social-realism trophy
we will win.

Every time I sit down for a poem
I've gotta get up for a dog's yelp.

First published in *Tripwire*, 18 September 2021.

Maung Yu Py

88 is like this, my kid brother

88 wasn't born yesterday, my kid brother.
88 isn't about the yellow fighting peacock sticker.
88 is a permanent scar branded with iron
on the chests of democracy warriors—
fallen students & survivors.

88 isn't the white mandarin collar shirt
you dare to wear only in fine weather.
88s are blood-drenched tunics
in the downpour of bullets
from the guns that "wouldn't shoot in the air."

To promote your name and party,
you hawk like a hawker.
88 isn't the voice from a loudspeaker with a permit.
88s are names that ooze out of the darkness
in the darkest of times,
the times when truth is cut with scissors and
blotted out with silver ink by the junta.

My kid brother, 88 isn't a fairy tale
that happened once upon a time
in the Kingdom of Varanasi.
88 really happened, twenty-five years ago,
on the road right in front of your house.

88s aren't those lies from the government paper,
attempting to conceal a dead elephant under a goat hide.
88s are historic photos featured
in international magazines and journals.

88 isn't an intact whitewashed wall.
88 is a wall from the past, its brickwork
laid bare with bullet holes and blood stains.

88 isn't a non-stop war action film.
88s are Bren Gun Careers, security forces,
batons, shields, tear gas canisters,
bombs, Enfield rifles, semi-automatic rifles, bayonets,
blue prison vans, barbed wires, steel jerry cans,
jinglee catapults loaded with sharpened bicycle spokes,
dahs, bamboo spikes, spears—lived experiences,
a struggle where people in the thousands
got murdered.

88 isn't a gang fracas, that broke out
all of a sudden, out of nowhere, out of madness.
88s were the waves of spirit of the whole of Burma
that inundated the streets, because
under the same old boots of the military tyranny
that kept changing its head, people could
no longer cope with their resentment.

88s weren't useless taung, plone bamboo baskets
that were trashed exactly because they were useless.
88s were more powerful than the Tatmadaw, and very
frightening for the authorities. They were heroes,
cut down like reed—even their roots were
dug out for good measure.

88 isn't an unneeded-outdated idea.
88 is a rice grain ghost that haunts in
the dreams of crony capitalists—
who are overfed with the junta's handout,
act like slave drivers to please their masters.

88 isn't a see-no-evil, hear-no-evil
ghost of history. 88 is fear out of the
brain-and-chest moulds of those
who had to make do with mediocre education
and a battered economy.

88 isn't a reading exercise in the subject of history
that has been censored out of school textbooks.
88 is a stone inscription all the people of Burma
know by heart.

Not that 88 has nothing to do with you, my kid brother.
88 is homework for life
you must study over and over …

Maung Yu Py was arrested at a protest in his hometown of Myeik in the extreme south of Myanmar on 8 March 2021. He was sentenced to two years imprisonment on 8 June 2021, and remained in Myeik prison as of January 2022.

Min Lu's poem

2010–1988

A poet has to live their times,
as if living were their occupation.

Aung Cheimt (1948–2021)

Hanthawaddy U Win Tin (1929–2014)

Fearless Tiger

translated by Kenneth Wong

Burning sun,
Pelting snow,
Sometimes the heat is prickly,
Sometimes the cold shakes me;
My narrow living quarter
Sees no bright light, feels no wind blow,
Sees no sunshine, nor no moonrise,
Sees no human, nor humanity.
Sit or gaze,
Sleep or think,
Can't get news, can't even sing a song,
Can't read, can't attempt poetry,
Can't preach, can't even speak to a soul.
Samsara is empty,
My world is tiny,
I pace in my little space,
I pause before the iron door,
I stand for a bit … and the day is gone.

Gone was the day before,
Gone is the whole today,
Gone will be the next day,
Gone, gone, gone …
Get them all gone!

A day or a life
A month or an age
A year or an era,
I won't lose hope, I won't give up,
Now I'm the anvil, later the hammer;
Don't you know
The truth is on my side,
The people are on my side,
Time stands by me,
And Buddha stands with me?

Do you think
I'll grow blunt in monotony
Like a caged tiger at the zoo?
What a laugh!

Remember!
As long as the black stripes
Cut across my yellow bright,
Unmistakable
And clear,
A tiger is a tiger,
And I am
Just the same!

Hanthawaddy U Win Tin (1929-2014)

Hell On Earth: A Collage

They fear him because he is incorruptible.
—Aung San Suu Kyi

I TURNED 80 TODAY. The crematorium is within sight for an octogenarian. Not very far. Not very far, I said. Don't ask, "How far?" Don't come tell me, "You have a long way to go." I know the final destination is near. I know the funeral pyre is on my premises. I know my days are numbered. I know death is close. Above all, I know I still have a lot of things to do. And I will do what I can.

For twenty years, I have seen and heard jail comedy, jail tragedy, jail gags and jail tears; dukkha in jail, anguish in jail, routine in jail, woes and worries in jail, appreciative joy at other people's wellbeing in jail, determination in jail, struggle in jail, political activism in jail, wisdom and knowledge in jail, transcendental state of mind in jail, the essence of jail, the look and the logic of jail and the biography of jail.

They ripped me of my housing entitlement when they sent me to jail. They ripped me of my pension and all other benefits. I lost all my teeth during the interrogation by Military Intelligence. I gummed jail food, coarse rice and boiled vegetables, simply to keep myself alive. For eight years. I can't describe my jail dukkha in words. I got gastritis in jail. For five years, they didn't treat my hernia. They didn't send me to hospital. They left me alone to rot. It was too late by the time my hernia was operated on. My internal organs were already crammed. They got too entangled with my nerves. The operation has left one of my thighs permanently in pain. I lost one of my testicles. Now my heart condition is sending me to the necropolis.

For twenty years, I was in an isolation cell. They cut me off from other political prisoners and criminal convicts. Let alone speaking with mates from the room next door, they couldn't hear me yell as there were three or four empty rooms (32 by 48 feet) between my cell and my neighbour's.

At 80, I have no home. No money. No head for thought. I have become a fucking blockhead. No strength for movement. A crippled old man with a series of diseases. No refuge. I can't even visit monasteries and pagodas, homes of friends and relatives, public gardens, offices, markets, museums, hospitals and graveyards on my own. I can't. I am always followed by informants on motorcycles.

As in Tin Moe's poem, I know my cheroot has burned down. I know the sun is brown. Yet I won't ask, "Will someone take me home?"

Whether or not the playing field is level, I still want to be on the pitch.

*

I turned 85 last month.

The other day doctors said they had successfully operated on my kidney. You never buy what doctors sell in this country. Since I turned 80, I've been more than prepared for this. They say I have multiple organ dysfunction syndrome (MODS). They have fixed me up on oxygen therapy. Doesn't Burma have MODS? Why don't they fix the country up with oxygen therapy?

I thank the painkillers. I thank my supporters, friends and comrades.

Don't keep me in wake. Bury me instantly.

Don't worry. I will see myself out.

Hell On Earth (2010, Democratic Voice of Burma) translated and collaged by Ko Ko Thett. "Great Guest" by Tin Moe, translation by Anna Allott.

Hanthawaddy U Win Tin was a veteran Burmese journalist, politician and political prisoner. He was one of the founding members of the National League for Democracy (NLD), and remained a staunch opponent to the Myanmar military regimes throughout his life. He was jailed for nineteen years (1989–2008) for his writings and his role in the NLD. After his release from prison in 2008, U Win Tin continued to wear a blue prison shirt as a sign of solidarity with his colleagues who remained in captivity. According to his autobiography, U Win Tin composed "Fearless Tiger" while still in captivity.

Min Ko Naing

Which song, my dear girl?

translated by Kenneth Wong

Which song should I teach you, my dear girl?
The sound of whips
All day long,
All for the sake of a pyramid—
Let not this kind of music
Be around in your time,
Don't want you to sing along,
Not even by accident.

For you and this era to sing together,
I blindly write
In my dream
A chorus
That makes all the pianos mute.

Can you hear the music
Of the rise and fall of rosary beads,
Of sunlight striking the pagoda gongs,
Of jasmine buds washing their hands,
Of snails pouting
And stomping their feet?
Just keep listening, my dear girl.

A flock of skylarks
Over my head;

Looks like they're heading home,
Turning in for the night.
Such a precious sight!
Daddy's still looking at them.

Written in Kyaingtong Prison, 2011.

Min Ko Naing

Drawing

translated by Kenneth Wong

Now that the pencil has been sharpened,
Draw a classroom,
Or a nude—
It's up to you.

Let this land
Be strewn with swords and spears,
Or be blessed by flying doves—
It's up to you.

I assure you, dear child,
If you look away
Because you hate battle scenes and bloody fights,
No one will call you a coward.

But, my child,
You must put your name
On whatever you choose to draw.

Min Ko Naing

The groom of fallen stars

a poem in tribute to Taya Min Wai, 1966–2007

translated by Kenneth Wong

1: My friend,
You nurtured your conviction
Like your own child.

2: My friend,
You
Burned your injuries like lamp oil.

3: My friend,
You
Could lick your own wounds
And resurrect.

4: My friend,
You had to
Drape your own skin,
Sharpen your bone into a needle,
Sew your own outfit,
And look marvelous in it.

5: Go ahead, my friend.
We must stay behind
To heal the best we can
The injuries of this world
Where the stars are falling, one by one.

6: Go ahead, my friend.
We must stay behind
To shield the earth's wounds
From the many scorching suns
With our bare hands.

7: Go ahead, my friend.
We must stay behind
To write your poetry's table of contents
On the world's vinyl record of grief.

8: Go ahead, my friend.
On the day the peacock banners
Fly once more along the campus wall
We shall ….

Former political prisoner and student leader Min Ko Naing regularly publishes his poetry on his Facebook page. In his verses, the reticent rebel leader often reveals his inner struggles, anxieties and hopes. After the February 2021 military coup, he reprises his previous role as a leading figure in the resistance movement.

Kyi May Kaung

They were just following orders

When it came to it no one could find out
where the orders came from all they knew was
they came from Above, not from the sky—
number One[1] blamed Two and Two blamed One.
The people blamed the Butcher[2]
but guns do not all on their own suddenly
spout death with bayonets and live bullets.

Someone somewhere had first of all to decide
the budget would go more to guns than to butter
or rather more guns and bullets than rice—
than food rationed even in the relatively better
times, a bottle of cooking oil for a family of four
per month, a bottle of kerosene in four months
barely enough to soak the torn and twisted corkscrew-like
newspaper to start the fire going—sometimes four minute
lighter flints wrapped in paper and damp-headed, dead-
headed, matches that never ignite. Then someone had to tell
all those soldiers to march five abreast
goose-stepping down the streets. Didn't you
see on Nightline, this young man just
looking around, just passing the time, sitting
on the street—shooting the breeze—inside a
spare tire—slim

---

1   A careful way of referring to General Ne Win.
2   The notorious street name of Sein Lwin, believed to have ordered
the 1988 shootings. Sein Lwin died destitute and out of favor in 2004.

protection—suddenly shot
Wham! In the chest.

Somewhere
all these soldiers with their fingers on the
triggers. During the Demonetisation[3] toting up
the numbers on punched cards, we did not
even dare to sneeze. Somewhere someone had
to say, it's time to shoot, it's OK to shoot
children, their jinglees,[4] sharpened bicycle spokes
were dangerous, they taunted
the soldiers, for their lack of education.
Does Provocation justify being shot?

And someone who should have known better
says to me in America—they were warned not
to come out—the army would shoot to kill
and yet they did. Whose fault is it? I
look on in horror—would you say this—if it
were your child? Your son? Now thirteen.
He says—But nothing happened
to the boy—Does that prove anything?

During the (first) Gulf War a man wrote to the

---

3   Over the years, the Burmese military government has tried to con-
trol its self-created inflation (they print too much money) by frequently
declaring over the radio that some denominations are no longer legal
tender. The first major demonetisation was in 1964, when all university
staff were assigned to help do the accounts inside Convocation Hall on
the Rangoon University campus. Since writing this poem, I have also
incorporated some of these episodes into my fiction.
4   A word that suddenly appeared in the summer of 1988, during the
height of the mass countrywide pro-democracy demonstrations, and
then just as suddenly disappeared.

President of the United States: Mr Bush[5] if
my son dies I will not forgive you. The
paramount leader says contemptuously
of his own people—with whom he wishes so
much to identify: They quickly forget
anyone who has wronged them, they quickly
forgive. But do you really think, the mother
of a 5'8" tall son, who came home, legs broken, in a 5' coffin, who
stays silent out of fear, has really forgiven?

How long do you think it takes to grow
a baby into a man, nurtured every day
from when his shoulders were two finger joints wide
the soles of his feet, two finger widths long?

I can't imagine how you could walk
that day in September. On the radio before
I left for the railway station, I heard, the mood
is very grim—the students are prepared to
die. Two and a half hours later as I get off the train in
Baltimore—my friend greeting me from
her little red car, says—It's all over, the army
has taken back power again, the students
have fled to the Border. My feet are like
jelly and walk along without any act of
volition on my part. My friend had stopped
to buy a pink anthurium, and had forgotten
behind one of her twenty credit cards.
She said her husband heard the news on
his shortwave radio.
Suddenly I think of Oświęcim in the

---

5   President George H W Bush.

winter, in February, the warehouses full
of women's hair, children's booties, suitcases,
pathetic names and addresses, written on each.
Spectacles all sorted out systematically by type.
Concrete slab tables used, to pull out the
gold fillings, before, the corpses are
incinerated. Even killing can be mass
production. Of hair, used to weave
upholstery. My classmate from
Nigeria writes a poem—of how all that hair
is now all a uniform colour because of the gas,
was once also different in colour, not just in
texture or was it curly or straight, short or
long—was once on some woman's head
who was once loved by some man. On the
way back from Auschwitz to Kraków, he shows
me the poem, on the bus.

In the Spring in Majdanek near Lublin
my friend takes me through a field of
yellow dandelions. We climb steps as up
a Burmese stupa. She says though it's a
lovely day, and we are on holiday, do
not smile for your picture. It is not
appropriate here, Elsbièta says. These are human
ashes—they only roofed it over recently.

How much human ashes must have
blown away in this open field between the War
and our visit in 1969? How much ash
does one human being make?
Ounces? Pounds? I think ounces. When

my other friend's father died and he was
cremated, she said she interred the
ashes in an urn. I should have looked.
How much ash does one human being—
produce?

Kyi May Kaung is a Burma-born political economist with a PhD from the University of Pennsylvania. She had worked to promote democracy in Burma as an exile activist over twenty years since 1997. She started writing poetry in the mid-1990s and is a winner of the William Carlos Williams Award of the Academy of American Poets. The poem, dated 1996, was written in English.

Myo Myint Nyein

Together with Ko Min Lu

TO BE HONEST I didn't have much gusto to write these events down. However, I have come across several misquotations and misreadings regarding the 1988 democracy movement. I am writing this simply to leave a record about the poem, "What's going on?", by Min Lu, and the poet's part in our rough road to democracy.

The 8 August 1988 (8888) uprising was preordained with fatal shootings. On 13 March 1988, a brawl broke out at the Sandar Win teashop near Rangoon Institute of Technology (RIT) in Insein Township, between some RIT students and a group of local youths from nearby East Gyogone neighbourhood, over the right of way to the teashop's cassette tape player. The brawl quickly turned into a communal clash between the students and the neighbourhood. The security forces intervened by beating up and opening fire on the students. Two students, Phone Maw and Soe Naing, were killed.

A student protest erupted the following day. On 16 March, when the police broke up a student rally, some students were beaten up again at the west bank of Inya Lake near Rangoon University. The police brutality only led to an escalation of student protests in June and July and, by August, the protests snowballed into a nationwide democracy uprising of peoples from all walks of life, including monks, artists, writers and filmmakers.

Ko Min Lu was one among them. He was also active in the 1974 student uprising and was jailed for some time along with many other student activists of that era. In the 8888 movement he was with an association of writers and artists and was one of the organisers of massive public forums in Rangoon on 22,

24 and 26 August, where Daw Aung San Suu Kyi, who would emerge as the opposition leader, was scheduled to speak.

Daw Suu was unable to attend the forum at the premises of Rangoon General Hospital (RGH) on 22 August. On 24 August, Daw Suu appeared, flanked by members of the writers and artists association, at the RGH to speak to members of the public—it was her political debut. As she faced several security issues, she didn't show up on time. She was nearly one-and-a-half hours late.

By the time Daw Suu arrived, writer U Win Khet, who was heading a rally starting at the RGH, already left with a massive column of people. Only a few writers and artists remained waiting for Daw Suu at the RGH. Ko Min Lu was one of them. Another public forum was scheduled on 26 August at the west arcade of Shwedagon Pagoda. In the afternoon of 25 August the Military Intelligence personnel (MI) began to hand out malicious statements about Daw Suu. It dawned on the forum organisers that Daw Suu's security must be a priority.

Ko Min Lu supervised the security operations. He solicited help from a Thinganyun-Yangon bus driver, who drove one of those fat-tummy buses, the wartime-era Chevy Field Artillery Tractors (FATs) locally repurposed into buses. He loaded the bus with car batteries to power an amplifier for horn loudspeakers.

His colleagues were assigned different tasks. Before the break of dawn on 26 August, a "minesweeping operation" was in progress on the western premises of Shwedagon. The minesweeping wasn't done with any modern instrument. Ko Min Lu's team just walked hand in hand all over the areas near the west arcade to see if anyone would step on a mine! The minesweepers decided to risk their lives, knowing well that, had there been an actual mine as rumour had it, they would have been killed. They risked their lives for a leader the country truly and urgently needed.

By eight in the morning, people in groups began to gather in front of the forum stage. Not long after that the whole area near the west stairway of Shwedagon was brimming with people. On the left side, in front of the stage was a fat tummy bus, with Ko Min Lu himself sitting firmly in the driver's seat. The bus was at the ready to blockade the stage in the event of an assassination attempt against Daw Suu or some other misfortunes. The people prevailed on that day. The forum was concluded without any mishaps. A unanimous decision to establish a new democratic nation was reached at the forum.

The National League for Democracy (NLD) was subsequently established. Just when the NLD started to embark on their campaigns, Daw Suu and a number of opposition leaders were arrested. With their chests held high, opposition leaders walked into jails, declaring "Martyrs' kin are immortal." Daw Suu was placed under house arrest. It was around that time, July 1989, a poem titled, "What's going on?" came out:

> "Aw ... dukkha, dukkha!
> It's not easy being a martyr
> under their thumb. Every Martyrs' Day
> one gets perfunctory salutes.
> "Under the guidance of Mr Chairman ..."
> used to be their line.
> Now that we've become a failed state
> General Aung San is the culprit.
> Even his own daughter is restricted
> from laying a wreath at his tomb."

The unsigned poem was widely distributed and promoted, especially by the "Tri-colour Student Group" at student meetings and rallies. There are three poems under the same title. The poet didn't want to be named. It was not unusual for poets to remain anonymous at that time. Being caught for writing a protest poem would mean long years in jail that would thwart their pro-democracy activities. The only exceptions were poets Tin Moe and Shwe Phone Lu.

Today some of the well-known protest poems copied and shared on the internet are attributed to the wrong authors. "A Matchstick", the poem that opens with the line "Twenty years, huh?", which was widely circulated when the dissident Maung Thawka was serving his twenty-year sentence in Insein prison, for instance, was written by the late female poet Ma Seine Pin, herself also a political prisoner. The controversial "If" by Rudyard Kipling was rendered into a beautiful Burmanised version by Ma Thida, not by Daw Aung San Suu Kyi as commonly assumed. "Back to School" was written by Shwe Phone Lu, who wrote under his better-known name Tayar Min Wai. There are several other "nameless" poems from that time, but I will not name the authors without getting their consent first.

For writing, publishing and distributing "What's going on?", Ko Min Lu, the Tri-Colour Student Group leader Ko Sein Hlaing, and I got a seven-year sentence each. Here I would like to recount a memorable anecdote. When I was interrogated at the MI-7 headquarters, I told them Ko Min Lu wrote the poem because I asked him to. Being the true poet that he was, he refuted my claim and said that he wrote what he wanted to write, and that nobody told him to write the poem. He took full responsibility and owned up to what he did.

He and I spent many days and nights in the same cell. As one of my comrades, he endured all sorts of hardship, repression and torture. It's been three years since he passed away. I am sharing this to mark Ko Min Lu's birthday with his fans to highlight just one of the many roles he played on our rough road to democracy.

The original essay "Ko Min Lu ne atu [Together with Ko Min Lu]" appeared as afterword by Myo Myint Nyein in *Min Lu: kabya paung chope* [Collected Poems by Min Lu], NDSP Books, Yangon (2018).

Yu Ya

Clarification on "What's going on?"
by Min Lu

"WHAT'S GOING ON?" was penned by Father, edited by Uncle Myo Myint Nyein, and distributed by Uncle Sein Hlaing. U Myo and U Sein Hlaing were detained first. They didn't squeal on Father. They didn't name the author. To what extent they must have been roughed up in jail, I cannot imagine. I learned from dad that even the Military Intelligence (MI) officer who arrested him acknowledged, "All three of you, your mouths are zipped!"

There was someone else. Besides dad and the two Uncles, someone else knew that dad wrote the poem. Acting on that person's tip, the MI arrested dad. Dad told me of that episode, but he never named him or her. No one is to blame.

"What's going on?" cost U Myo Myint Nyein and U Sein Hlaing seven years each in jail. Dad, owing to a number of reasons, was released after two years. One of those reasons was that he signed a pledge that he would never get involved in politics again. Both Uncles were supportive of dad's decision, "You have small children. Your wife Ma Shan doesn't even raise her voice. What you did is right."

U Myo and U Sein Hlaing received some additional years on top of their seven years in jail. Perhaps that's why dad hardly talked about his time in jail. He never wrote about it either. Dad must have felt that he didn't fulfil his duty. I saw how overjoyed he was on the day U Myo and U Sein Hlaing were released from jail.

Above all—I don't know who started it, but there's an

anecdote about dad's arrest. The story goes, when the MI officer came to take him away, dad declined to wear the hood they put on him, and requested that he use his own, something he had tailored for his own head just in case.

That story has been making rounds for a while now. Nothing could be further from the truth. If I don't clarify it, it might be taken as a fact. Some writers, such as Okka Kyi Win, have echoed that anecdote in writing in admiration of dad.

I thank them, but I would like to make things clear; it was around 11 pm when they came to our house to take dad away. Dad just went along with them in the clothes he was wearing that night, leaving everything behind. He didn't do what we often see in the films; he didn't bid farewell to his children. Nor did he say, "Don't worry, I will be back soon." Just like many other politicians who were used to being taken away, he was taken away. Nothing special. Fortunately, he wasn't tortured as badly as Uncle Myo or Uncle Sein Hlaing.

"What's Going On?" is a triptych. The poem, written in post-coup Burma in 1989, has made a comeback in post-coup Myanmar in 2021. It is widely shared on social media. I am grateful about that. I would just like to make a humble request. Please do not share the poem to degrade anyone. I believe dad would have said the same. The poem should be shared in dad's memory.

Finally, if I may add, when it comes to the events surrounding this particular poem, I have more respect for U Myo and U Sein Hlaing than I have for my dad. My huge respect also goes to the students who wound up in jail for handing out copies of dad's poem.

Dad kept going on about how he didn't have to go through what the two Uncles and the students went through in jail.

My conscience reflects my dad's.

Min Lu (1954–2013)

What's going on?

I.
I hear the children sing,
"You shouldn't step over
your own mother to embrace the big aunt.
You may walk over your own father
to hug your Paukphaw from China.
Attention! Fire brigades, navy and airforce!
Only the Tatmadaw will rake in
all national profits."
Even the children couldn't help.
You must file a complaint at
the State Law and Order Restoration Council!

What's going on?
Too many rumours.
No one was killed at Inya Lake.
People were just beaten up with
rubber batons, shot with rubber bullets,
and stabbed with rubber bayonets.
O … haven't we come of age
in the Age of Rubber?

What's going on?
Burma has been renamed Myanmar.
Ms Burma is Ms Myanmar now.
We Bamar Association has become
We Myanmar Association.

Good thing the 1st Earl Mountbatten of Burma
passed away before all that.

What's going on?
In the auction for jail terms,
the starting bid is three years.
A bidder, who yelled, "I want
to see a graceful Tatmadaw," won
a wholesome twenty years.
Tell me about it!
Even the Shwedagon Pagoda
is placed under probation
for a criminal offence.

What's going on?
In the State Law and Order Restoration Council
for Literature, the chap in green specs
takes the chair.
Uncle Tom is his deputy.
O … while our fellow writers
can't get any sleep because of bedbugs
someone is dreaming pink
in the Red Chamber, someone who
will scoop up ten thousand kyat
when everyone else gets a thousand.
Will he climb over the mountain of bones
and swim across the sea of blood?

What's going on?
Don't you believe
the big man has retired?
It's real. These days

he only handles
military and business affairs.

What's going on?
The three objectives of National Day are
- You shall not wear homespun pinni
- You shall not hang the portrait of General Aung San
- You shall not scream, "Our cause, our cause!"
Even under the colonial rule
there were anti-colonial rallies.
There was the right to scream.
In the past
we were colonised by others.
These days we are colonised by ourselves.

What's going on?
A student was expelled because
he wore a black yaw longyi to class.
We aren't supposed to grieve on any anniversary.
If you miss your fallen friends
you will face charges
under the law against longing.
"Students are impolite.
They do not respect the elders," say
the people who wear boots on religious premises.
These same people wouldn't take off their gun belts
even when offering waso robes to the sangha.

What's going on?
"Basic Law of Union of Burma" should be read
at least once in a lifetime?
Is it as good as Shwe Mi cheroots,

selling as many copies as exercise books and
as popular as chai lottery?
What's going on?
I am giving a marathon speech because
I don't have time for short talks.
The man who doesn't know the distinction
between "konthweiyay [trade]" and "kontike [shopping
    mall]" is the chairperson
and the man who tends to forget the very day
he staged a coup is Secretary One of
The State Law and Order Restoration Council.
Oh … these are the times—
headless people are decking themselves out in hats!

What's going on?
What's going on?
What's going on?

II.
Aw … dukkha, dukkha!
It's not easy being a martyr
under their thumb. Every Martyrs' Day
one gets perfunctory salutes.
"Under the guidance of Mr Chairman …"
used to be their line.
Now that we've become a failed state
General Aung San is the culprit.
Even his own daughter is restricted
from laying a wreath at his tomb.

For occupying the Shwedagon wuttaka land
even the mausoleum could have been

relocated in Hlaingthaya.
We are *almost* grateful they haven't come to that!

The Tatmadaw that loves the country,
the patriotic Tatmadaw,
the Tatmadaw, the protector of the people,
the Tatmadaw, the defender of Burma,
the fucking brilliant Tatmadaw …
the Tatmadaw that hisses with
a flair of cleverness, taw taw taw!

Look how the so-called squatters were
resettled in new homes, replete with water and fire.
In the monsoon, their homes get flooded.
In the dry season, their homes catch fire.
That's what I call "water and fire".
Democratic monks are labelled
"robe wearers" by none other than
the people who wear trousers.
Then again, they are buying off
the monks with waso robes.

"I am waging war to end wars,"
said Mr Secretary, the storyteller.
Where did I hear that before?
Ronald Reagan said something similar
in defence of Star Wars, it occurred to me.
Look, Reagan's bollocks are in his mouth!

"As the senior journalists know
if we don't do this, that will happen,
if we don't do that, this will happen,

and therefore,
we would like you to do this and that."
so goes the press release from
The Committee for Timely News!
The pressed release! Do you get it?

That one, Secretary One, or whatever,
who likes to greet whoever he meets with,
"How are you?", he is in the habit of
pointing his index finger here and there.
He doesn't have a clue, wherever
his finger is pointed at, dukkha happens.
Here comes the chair of
National Gardens Construction Committee!
Giving speeches is his favourite pastime.

"I don't want to say this, but I should say
what I ought to say. What I ought to say
is that I don't want to say this."
How remarkable!
"Our government is legitimate
and recognised by the international community."
He is right.
The government is unanimously recognised as
the most spineless government in the world!

"Do it accurately, correctly and swiftly"
except for the constitution and transfer of power.
Basic law is not like martial law.
It can't be issued overnight.
Transfer of power is not like a power putsch.
It can't be done in a shoddy manner.

And yet …
there will be a power transfer
there will be a power transfer
just like the power is being transferred
when rocking a cradle.
He suggests, "Study Dr Maung Maung."
Read "Basic Law of Union of Burma" by Sayar Maung Maung.
He keeps banging on about it!
If you are selling the book, I suggest,
the book should be served with
a complimentary packet of
Sayar Maung brand red herbal powder.
The book sale will go through the roofs.

Wait a minute
why do you have to grin
every time you give a speech?
It scares me.
Reminds me of an old verse that goes like
"bilu monster's fangs are fucking exposed …"

By way of a conclusion, shouldn't you say,
the three ultimately urgent causes of the Tatmadaw are—
"We shall safeguard our Godfather."
"We shall safeguard our Godfather."
"We shall safeguard our Godfather."

Ouch …
What's going on?

III.
In Burma
the one-party system has been dismantled.
And yet "The Working People's Pickle Daily"
continues to rule as the one and only
dictatorial paper.
Not a single report in the paper is true
some readers say.
It's not that bad.
At least one report is 50 percent accurate—
the weather report.
Once a month
there's a column that's 100 percent spot on—
the lottery results.

"When it comes to the love of one's country
I can compete with anyone," Mr Secretary claims.
I trust you, Mr Secretary. I trust you.
Your love for
Pyinlon gem fields is proof enough
of your love for the country.

"Military can rule the country with martial law.
Civilians must first have a new constitution
to form a government."
Wait a sec!
Who's mandated you with the so-called martial law?
You've issued it for yourself,
haven't you?
If that's the case
cannot students empower themselves with
"student law"?

"Only 30 percent of the population
support the opposition party."
True, if you include children, who
are not of voting age, in the population.
Using your maths, I can say,
only 40 percent of the population would have approved
the Burma Socialist Programme Party in the 1974 referendum.
What's the percentage of the population that supports the junta th
How few?

In drafting the new constitution,
you said, you'd have to consult with
all of the "135 ethnic national races".
Did you consult with the ethnic groups
before you staged the army coup?

"The State Law and Order Restoration Council
is like a football referee. A referee will only administer
the Laws of the Game. He will not take part in the game,"
you said. Perhaps you are talking about
the chai lottery referee? O …Senior General of Referee,
Even a lottery referee
will give out the money to the winners
"accurately, correctly and swiftly".

Listen, public clamours resound,
"Immediately release all political prisoners!
Immediately transfer power!"
The whole world could hear us.
Are you pretending to be deaf?
Haven't you heard of the Hebrew scripture,
"Whoever shuts their ears to the cry of

the poor will also cry out and not be answered."

"We are not cowed by threats from powerful nations.
We are not scared of Nuremberg Trials."
Maybe, you've already packed and set out
a flight path to safety. Only your underlings
will be left dying like mutts and swines.
Haven't you heard of,
"The way of the wicked is darkness.
They know not as they stumble."

Now you say this. A moment later you say that.
You forbid us to do this. You forbid us to say that.
Decrees are often issued. Press conferences often held
to repeat your lies. Don't you know,
"As a dog returns to its own vomit,
so fools repeat their folly."

"Tell this to Awara ..." you command,
"Tell him to watch what he says.
If not, he will face a trial."
What an edict!

Haven't you marked the Lord Buddha's words,
"As dust thrown against the wind, mischief
is thrown back in the face of the fools
who wrong the pure and harmless" ?

Whatever happens,
we must not lose sight of our three national causes—

1. Steer clear of the State Law and Order Restoration

Council
2. Befriend the student activists and learn from them
3. May the people and the monks be able to lend a hand

That's the way of the fighting peacock,
the way for an auspicious land!

Aung Cheimt (1948-2021)

from Gandawin Ma Ma

10.

That person
                will enter
from behind the divider.

Perhaps from the asphalt road,
        humming a song,
                he's walking through words.

Button up your shirt.
                        shut your windows,
shut your moon, shut your sun!
Sleepless?
To keep the heartbeats lukewarm
there are tiny pill bottles.

        My heart won't beat for you.
I won't be thrilled with you.
        Shut your door in high pitch UGAHHH!

O… even my shadows are
shattered   &   fragmented.
My wound, gushing blood,
complains to everyone in sight —

office clerks & envelope pushers,
porters at the port,
railroad workers,

sailors,
students, soldiers,
girls rolling cheroots on a daily wage &
hawkers carrying their wares on their shoulders.
               O…all the peasants & farmers
          I speak to you as the matter arises,
all the doors have been shut on me.

Isn't it a crime
not to love each other?

Shouldn't the Act 420
for imposture & forgery
apply to self-deceit?
I will climb to the top of the world
to present
these bullet points.

"Gandawin Ma Ma", inspired by "A Cloud in Trousers" by Vladimir Mayakovsky, translated into Burmese from English by Maung Tha Noe, comprises twelve parts. Presented here is Part 10, where the poet refers to himself in the third person [That man …] as well as in the first person. Mayakovsky's unrequited love was Maria Denisova, Aung Cheimt's was a lady he called "Gandawin Ma Ma". Gandawin denotes traditional or classical Burmese literature, music or arts. Ma Ma is a term of endearment for a lady lover, older than oneself. Gandawin Ma Ma, therefore, would have been a lady of traditional poise and deportment. The poem, however, was dedicated to poet Phaw Way (1944–1978). Written in 1974, the poem is considered a watershed in the modernist "khitpor" vanguard, espoused by Aung Chemit, Phaw Way, Maung Chaw Nwe and Thukamaing Hlaing. Since its first publication in 1979, the poem has been reprinted at least six times.

Aung Cheimt, passed away from suspected stomach ulcer at his home in Yangon on 9 August 2021. He was not properly diagnosed at North Okkalapa hospital, which was understaffed due to the strike by medical professionals.

Maung Chaw Nwe (1949–2002)

To wilt is to bloom

translated by Kenneth Wong

For flowers,
To wilt is to bloom.
If you pluck one
One more rises.
If you drop two
Two more spring up.

Come! Knock us down,
Wild gust; tumble us,
Cut us down, storming blades,
Blow your hardest, do your worst.
Litter the ground with our buds,
Trample on us, see if we care.

To wilt is to bloom,
That's the flowers' doctrine.
You may crush us, we may fall,
But when we die we rise again.

Notorious as a flamboyant, troubadour-like poet, Maung Chaw Nwe once famously declared: "I've never thought of living life in moderation." To him, poetry is "a karmic disorder and a leprosy of retribution." His untimely death in 2002 was one of the most tragic events of the decade for his contemporaries and fans. He is survived by his wife, Myint Myint Sein, and three children. His work remains extremely popular and can be seen to have had a great influence in developing a new generation of readers and writers of Burmese poetry.

Epilogue

Min Nyein Aye

Map of Myanmar

All that remain are
a pebble in my fist,
a water bottle in my backpack &
a heap of bones.

"What's next?"
they asked.
"No next"
I answered.

No need to climb
the mountains of the past.
No need to row towards
the rivers & rivulets of the past.

The sacred text says
there is a whetstone here;
There is natural gas there.

"What's next?"
they asked.
"No next"
I answered.

For a clue
I will leave this poem
so you can work out
the depth & the breadth
of the country.

First published in Burmese at moemaka.com

Acknowledgments

This book is a culmination of not-for-profit efforts and generous contributions of time and labour by all parties concerned; poets, essayists, translators, and not least our colleagues at Ethos Books. We are very grateful that Ethos Books was able to accommodate our vision and demands for this anthology.

We are grateful to Emily Fishbein, Win Myat Nyein, Mayco Naing, Mayyu Ali, Ma Thida and Anna Allott for their guidance and moral support.

Ko Ko Thett is grateful to the editors and publishers of *Adi Magazine*, *Asia Literary Review*, *Cha Literary Journal*, *Cimarron Review*, *Cyphers Magazine*, *Index on Censorship*, *Jacket2*, *Los Angeles Review of Books*, *Mekong Review*, *Modern Poetry in Translation*, *Poetry International*, *PR&TA*, *Tripwire Journal*, *Usawa Literary Review* and *Voice & Verse* for featuring his translations of Burmese poems and two of his obituary pieces from 2014 to 2021. Special thanks to the Burmese magazines and publishers, *Tharaphu*, *Hninsi Phyu*, The Eras and NDSP. Very special thanks to *Moemaka* online journal for making witness poetry and essays from Myanmar a prominent feature in 2021. This book would not have been possible without the other Thett.

Unless otherwise mentioned, all poems and essays are translated from Burmese by Ko Ko Thett.

Additional Translators:
Kenneth Wong is the author of *A Prayer for Burma* (Santa Monica Press), *Easy Burmese* (Tuttle Publishing), and *Survival Burmese* (Tuttle Publishing). His writings, short stories, essays and poetry translations have appeared in *AGNI*, *Grain*, *San Francisco*

Chronicles, *Myanmar Times*, *The Irrawaddy* and *Mekong Review*, among others. He currently teaches beginning and intermediate Burmese at the University of California, Berkeley.

Thett Su San is a Burmese literary translator with a speciality in contemporary women fiction. As of 2022, she serves as curator and series editor for a chapbook series of Burmese short stories in English translation for Strangers Press. She holds an MA in Literary Translation from University of East Anglia, UK.

*

Essay translated by Thett Su San

Whose footfall is loudest	Thawda Aye Lei

Poems translated by Kenneth Wong

Fearless Tiger	Hanthawaddy U Win Tin
Which song, my dear girl?	Min Ko Naing
Drawing	Min Ko Naing
The groom of fallen stars	Min Ko Naing
To wilt is to bloom	Maung Chaw Nwe

List of works written in English:

Section 1

Myanmar	Zeyar Lynn
Two words I hate most	Dialogue Partner
Picking off new shoots will not stop the spring	Ma Thida
Sister Nu Tawng: Extraordinary courage out of everyday kindness	Nhkum Lu
My story	Ningja Khon
Drone paints	Poet of No Identity

About the Editors

Ko Ko Thett is a Burma-born poet, literary translator, and poetry editor for *Mekong Review*. He started writing poems for samizdat pamphlets at the Yangon Institute of Technology in the '90s. After a brush with the authorities in the 1996 student protest, and a brief detention, he left Burma in 1997 and has led an itinerant life ever since. Thett has published and edited several collections of poetry and translations in both Burmese and English. His poems are widely translated and anthologised. His translation work has been recognised with an English PEN award. Thett's most recent poetry collection is *Bamboophobia* (Zephyr Press, 2022). He lives in Norwich, UK.

Brian Haman is a researcher and lecturer in the department of English and American Studies at the University of Vienna. He completed his PhD in literature at the University of Warwick (UK) and has studied or held research appointments in Europe, China and the US. A book, art and music critic, he writes widely on contemporary culture from Asia, and, since 2017, has been an editor of *The Shanghai Literary Review*. His forthcoming books include an anthology of contemporary Chinese-language poetry in translation as well as an edition of the unpublished works of exiled Austrian Jewish writer Mark Siegelberg.

About this project

Picking off new shoots will not stop the spring is a multi-publisher, not-for-profit collaboration that aims to amplify the voices of the Burmese people alongside the ongoing Civil Disobedience Movement. If you are a publisher or reader keen on supporting this initiative, please visit **bit.ly/pickingoffnewshoots** for more details. The ebook of this title is also available free-of-charge for you to share their stories as widely as possible.